Once Upon a Time

Ye see yon birkie ca'd a lord,
Wha struts, an' stares, an' a' that,
Tho' hundreds worship at his word,
He's but a coof for a' that.
For a' that, an' a' that,
His ribband, star, an' a' that,
The man o' independent mind,
He looks an' laughs at a' that.

A Man's a Man for a' that by Robert Burns.

Copyright and Warning

Copyright © Sean T. Rassleagh, 2022.

The moral right of Sean T. Rassleagh to be identified as the author of this work has been asserted.

Once Upon a Time in Holyrood is a work of fiction. The novel is set many years in the future and some scenes are set in historic buildings. No connection between the fictional occupiers of premises in the novel and the present or previous occupiers of premises in real life is intended or should be inferred.

There is no correspondence between characters in the novel and real world people or families, living or dead, and none should be inferred. Some characters are partly inspired by characters in the novel 'Pride and Prejudice', the play 'Macbeth' and the poem 'Laird of Cockpen'.

Nothing in the novel should be taken as a factual statement about real world events, people, businesses or organisations.

All rights reserved.

Cover design by Rafael Andres.

Warning

The International Brotherhood of Sensitivity Readers, Local 1824 has given this book a rating of: FOUR CUDDLY KITTENS.

You are advised not to proceed further without appropriate emotional support animals.

In addition, chapter four has been determined to constitute a spill hazard.

If you are coming to this before reading the previous novels in the series a useful spoiler-free catch up is provided as an extra section at the end of the book.

The Bunnets

It is a truth universally acknowledged that one should never trust a Tory. Mrs Bunnet had cause to meditate on this fact once again as she stood in the rain with her five daughters at the bus stop on Niddrie Mains Road. It was six a.m. and all six ladies were wearing the green uniform of the City Farm, for they were on their way to the milking parlour. The financial predicament which had led to this unfortunate situation was, in Mrs Bunnet's opinion, solely due to the iniquity of Tories in England who had, a few months before, and only twenty-five years after independence excluded Scottish peers from the House of Lords and removed their allowances and pensions.

Admittedly, it had been many years since either Mrs Bunnet or her husband, Mr Bunnet, had attended the Lords. In her case, this resulted from a difference of opinion with the Procurer Fiscal, which had resulted in the confiscation of her passport. In her husband's case, non attendance was caused by senility and urinary incontinence. But that, considered Mrs Bunnet, was beside the point. A life peerage was supposed to be a sinecure. Their peerages were a reward for services already rendered, and they had, without a doubt, been treated shamefully.

The Bunnets were plain-spoken people who had reached an exalted position in life through good old-fashioned hard work, graft, and treason. Mrs Bunnet had grown up in one of the rougher parts of Glasgow. After failing her school exams, she had taken the first step into the world of business by the simple expedient of lying about her qualifications. Her first job was as an events manager for a beer manufacturer. The organisational skills she gained while organising piss-ups in their brewery provided a sound grounding and, after her employer dispensed with her services, she struck out on her own account as an underwear entrepreneur.

Mrs Bunnet's rumination on the perfidy of her former colleagues was brought to a halt by the arrival of her bus. The Bunnets alighted from the vehicle on South Bridge and walked along Chambers Street towards the courts. As was her habit, Mrs Bunnet muttered a curse and spat in the gutter as they crossed over Alex Salmond bridge, before passing Greyfriars Bobby and making their way down Candlemaker Row to Merchant Street. Two queues had formed at the service entrance to the courts complex: the first in the green uniform of the City Farm and the second in the classic navy blue of the Brothel. Almost everyone in the queues was female. Either biologically so or identifying as such, since the justice system did not favour maintaining a male identity. The doors opened, and the queues started to move just as they arrived: they were regulars and had their daily visit to the milking parlour, timed to perfection. Justice Elaine Cockburn arrived a few seconds after them. She too was a regular and a familiar face to the Bunnets.

"Hello Elaine," said Mrs Bunnet.

"Good morning, ladies," said Elaine, addressing the entire Bunnet family. "Anything interesting planned for today?"

The enquiry fell on welcoming ears. "We're going to the palace later," replied Mrs Bunnet. "I have an appointment to present the girls at court."

Elaine was suitably impressed by this intelligence.

"Aren't you presenting your daughter this year, too?" enquired Mrs Bunnet. "I thought she was the same age as my Lydia."

"Hestia isn't in Edinburgh. She went abroad to study genetic engineering." said Elaine. Then, somewhat more bitterly, she added, "In any case, she's not eligible, as her parents are not members of the aristocracy."

"Well, good luck to her! I'm sure she'll do very well. I'm afraid mine never had the brains for science. But why isn't she eligible? You're a Supreme Court justice. Surely they made you a baroness?"

"Unfortunately for me, all new titles are on hold until the government's commission on the future of the aristocracy and monarchy reports back."

"That's disgraceful!" said Mrs Bunnet. "But I'm sure it will work out in the end. The Tories have been doing better recently. If they get in all this republican nonsense will be stopped in its tracks and you'll get your title."

"It's hard to believe there's a real chance of a Tory becoming First Minister," said Elaine. "I have to admit their new man's rebranding as Pàrtaidh Tòraidheach na h-Alba to break with their unionist heritage was clever."

"Did you know the word Tòraidhe means robber?" said Mary. "I looked it up."

Mrs Bunnet frowned at her daughter and Elaine changed the subject to a less contentious topic.

"Looking forward to the Highland Show, girls?" she asked, turning to the Bunnet sisters.

Miss Jane Bunnett, the eldest sister, replied in the affirmative on behalf of her siblings.

Elaine was about to make further polite conversation about the debutante season. However, the queue had been moving forward as they conversed and, as they approached the door of the milking parlour, the farm's computers reconfigured their MedChips to make them more amenable as livestock. As a consequence, talking was impossible and they no longer had the use of their fingers. Human milk had become a valuable commodity after the UN was forced to take radical steps to mitigate climate change and farming animals had been banned. The rich were willing to pay good money for milk products and the government, which was continually strapped for cash, had seen a potential source of income from the penal system.

"Moooo!" said Elaine.

"Moo!" said Mrs Bunnet to show she was in the same boat.

The milkmaids fitted them with collars and led them to milking posts next to each other. The milking parlour was a friendly place, breasts were full and aching and the milking was a pleasant relief. Most of the staff were inmates and had been milked themselves just before opening the doors. Elaine slipped her hands and feet through the leather cuffs that would bind her to the post and waited for the milkmaid to buckle them shut. The posts and cuffs were theatre for the benefit of customers in the cafe above who could look down through the glass floor and see the milk for their extortionately overpriced Caffè latte being produced. She closed her eyes and relaxed as the front of her dress was unbuttoned and the cups fitted. Then came the familiar sound of the pump and the sensation of her milk flowing.

The pump gurgled as it increased suction to extract the last of the milk.

"Moo!" said Elaine to attract the attention of the milkmaid, who returned to switch off the pump and unbuckle the cuffs.

"Good job today, Elaine," she said, checking the notes on her iPad, "50 millilitres more than yesterday. Do you want to pay the milking fee and keep the produce yourself, same as usual?"

Elaine nodded.

"I'll put it aside in the fridge for you. Come and collect it whenever you like."

Elaine waited until she was led to the door of the parlour and her MedChip switched back to normal settings before replying.

"Thanks Stephanie, I'll collect after work, this afternoon."

"Sure thing, no problem, have a good day!"

Elaine was about to reply, but Stephanie had turned away and was putting a collar on the lady at the head of the queue.

The Bunnets were already finished and waiting just outside the parlour.

"Fifty millilitres extra today!" said Elaine with pride.

Mrs Bunnet said nothing. Her milk production was falling. For years her ample bosoms had provided a useful supplementary income to the family, and since the perfidious English had cut off her House of Lords allowances, an essential one. But age was catching up with her and the medications used to stimulate milk production were becoming less effective with time. She knew she was on the path to retirement. 'Retirement' was a pleasant enough word, but the reality was less so. For a criminal with a large debt to pay off, failing to keep up with the interest payments could mean one morning being herded into the butchers rather than the milking parlour. She needed to find wealthy husbands for her daughters, and it needed to be done in this year's social season.

— ♦ —

After leaving the parlour, Elaine said her goodbyes to the Bunnets and scanned her iris to enter the staff only section of the courts complex. Her chambers were some distance away in a historic section of the building near the Signet Library. The Bunnets, on the other hand, made their way back to the service entrance, where they joined the short queue waiting to enter His Majesty's Brothel. Mrs Bunnet had arranged to rent five white wedding dresses from the Brothel's costumier for the use of her daughters. It was common for debutantes to use the same dress for their presentation at court as their marriage later in the season. Both events required formal white dresses and only minor alterations were needed. The Brothel's dresses were particularly suitable since the tailoring made extensive use of velcro, which aided not only customisation for different eventualities but also rapid removal. Mrs Bunnet had selected the VIP version of the 'Wedding Night Experience' costume and was certain they would pass muster against the haute couture of the other debutantes.

The Bunnets were approaching the brothel commissary when they encountered the Madame herself walking in the opposite direction. It was unusual, but not unprecedented, to see the Madame in Brothel facilities, for although she now managed a multinational enterprise she also liked to keep her hand in: a preference partially explained by her regular consumption of the Brothel's version of Fuel. Brothel Fuel, like the standard Fuel supplied by the NHS contained a carefully balanced selection of nutrients tailored to an individual's needs, but it tasted far better than the normal Fuel and it complemented the nutrients with pharmaceuticals designed to create a feeling of wellbeing and a substantially increased work ethic in Brothel employees. Once you started to take it, it was difficult to stop, even if you knew what was in it.

"Ah, Mrs Bunnet, and your lovely daughters too," said the Madame. "Just the people I wanted to see! Let's borrow the costumier's office for a few minutes."

Mrs Bunnet suspected her day was about to take a turn for the worse; she could think of no favourable reason for the Madame looking for her.

The Madame sat behind the small metal desk, Mrs Bunnet took the guest chair on the other side of the desk and the five Bunnet sisters crowded into the small office behind their mother, pressing against the racks of clothing.

"Don't look so worried," said the Madame, "you're not in any trouble, I've got an opportunity that I want to discuss with you."

Mrs Bunnet attempted a smile.

"What did you wish to discuss, Madame?"

"Mrs Bunnet, you have five beautiful daughters. I would be delighted to employ any of them. But they are worth more as a set."

"Sorry?"

"Your youngest, Lydia, she will turn eighteen in September?"

"Yes, Madame."

"As I said, I would take any of them, but the full set is worth more."

"I don't follow."

"I'm looking for a first prize for the Brothel Lottery in October. A prize of five virgin sisters is unheard of: it would sell millions of tickets. I will offer one million euro for their services for 24 hours following the October Brothel draw, including the worldwide TV rights."

Mrs Bunnet was flabbergasted.

"One million euro!"

"Yes, as I said, I pay more for the set."

It was a generous offer, but after a few seconds' consideration, Mrs Bunnet stuck with her original plan.

"I'm sorry, Madame, but they are not for sale. Today they will be introduced at court and I expect them all to make excellent marriages this season."

The Madame smiled, "I was wondering who the five wedding dresses on that rack were for. Well, it's bad news for me, but I wish you all the best of luck with your matrimonial prospects. I hope the dresses are useful. It's always nice when our alumni enter the aristocracy: usually it is the other way round!"

Mrs Bunnet thanked the Madame for her good wishes and stood up to leave.

"Just a second, Mrs Bunnet. Let me have a quick look at your file before you go and see if there's anything else we should discuss."

The Madame logged in to the terminal on the costumier's desk.

"Oh, that's not so good," she muttered, "hmm, well then, that puts a different light on things."

She looked up.

"You'll appreciate I rarely get involved in the details of individual employees' loan accounts. But from the looks of it your arrears are increasing month to month, your milk production is dropping and your payments have been decreasing. It is not a good situation."

"I expect the loan to be cleared as soon as my daughters marry," said Mrs Bunnet. "The financial aspect will be raised with any potential suitors."

"I see," said the Madame, "well, it is up to you, but from what I see here I doubt the marriages will happen quickly enough. The credit decisions are automated and at the rate your arrears are growing, the City Farm's computer will almost certainly foreclose next month. Also, if you are retired from the dairy herd and sold for meat, it will raise nothing like enough to cover your debt and your family will inherit the remaining liability."

Mrs Bunnet hadn't realised the situation was so urgent. She gasped and started to cry. The Madame passed her a tissue from a box on the costumier's desk.

"Calm yourself, Mrs Bunnet. There's an easy enough solution. If your daughters agree to act as guarantors on your loan, I can intervene and put your account on hold until the end of September. If your daughters are married in time, then the account is closed and everyone is happy. Otherwise, the loan will be foreclosed, but instead of sending you to the butcher, the guarantors will become the prize in the October lottery. Twenty-four hours' work and the debt is repaid with another half million to split between them."

"We would inherit mum's unpaid debt anyway," said Jane, as usual speaking for all the sisters. "Of course we will be guarantors for her loan."

"Excellent!" said the Madame. "There will be a few standard conditions on the guarantors to reduce the Brothel's risk. It's just boilerplate. First, you must all wear one of our bracelets, second you may not leave the City of Edinburgh without obtaining permission, and third, the guarantors' liability is joint and several. Also, the one million euro offer is conditional on all five of you being virgins."

"Jesus!" said Jane, "that's as bad as the guarantor agreement to rent a flat."

The Madame smirked.

"If you think this agreement is bad, you should see our NDA."

— ♦ —

Mrs Bunnet's daughters changed into their rented frocks in the Brothel locker room and made their way down the Royal Mile towards Holyrood. They stuffed the hats, veils and trains which would be necessary at the palace but were superfluous at present into Tesco carrier bags for the walk. Mrs Bunnet herself had changed into a designer dress she had purchased in her younger and more affluent days. They passed St. Giles and came to the Heart of Midlothian mosaic in the pavement which marked the site of the Old Tolbooth prison. In their early years, their father had lectured the Bunnet sisters at length on the momentous historical significance of this sacred spot. It was this mosaic which had leant its name to a dance hall frequented by the founders of Heart of Midlothian FC, after which they had named the club. While followers of Hibs might spit in the centre of the mosaic for luck, Mr Bunnet had taught his daughters a more respectful tradition.

Mrs Bunnet stood to one side while they carried it out: as a native of Glasgow, her footballing allegiances were elsewhere. The girls linked hands and formed a circle around the mosaic, softly chanting "Na na na - nananana - nananana - Jam Tarts." After three choruses, Jane, as the eldest, led the solemn benediction.

"And when my life is over,
And when it has left its mark,
You can scatter all my ashes,
On the slopes of Tynecastle Park."

After a moment's silent reflection, the Bunnets continued on their way: their initial destination was a whitewashed Georgian villa set in its own grounds just off the Canongate. Once it had been the manse for Canongate Kirk but it was currently let to Lady Catherine Bampot who had generously made it available to Jack McCallister, leader of the Pàrtaidh Tòraidheach na h-Alba. The old manse was sandwiched between blocks of flats dating to the middle of the twentieth century and separated from the busy Canongate by a low wall and a meticulously kept garden with a lawn surrounded by rose bushes. Mrs Bunnet was about to ring the bell when she heard someone on the patch of grass at the side of the manse. A young man was playing with a football against the side of the building and making his own commentary.

"It's Ross, Ross with the ball, Ross for Murray and he shoots..."

But Ross did not shoot. Kitty had kicked her heels off, run over, tackled him and was now utilising the dribbling skills acquired in the school playgrounds of Craigmillar and Niddrie to keep the ball just outside his reach.

"Kitty!" said Mrs Bunnet. "Give the man his ball back!"

Ross Murray picked up the ball and surveyed the party.

"Are you the Bunnets?" he asked. "Mr McAllister is expecting you."

At that moment, a narrow red door in the side of the house opened and Mr McCallister himself appeared. He was a tall, thin man of about fifty with a stern face, tweed suit, starched shirt and carefully knotted tie. He ushered the ladies into the sitting room whose sash and case windows commanded a pleasant view over the front garden. The building smelled of fresh paint, but the furniture was antique and had been rented with the house.

"Good morning, ladies," said their host. "Welcome to Canongate Manse. I expect you will all have had your tea?"

The ladies were, in point of fact, quite thirsty.

"I could go a pint," said Lydia. "The farm just had a litre of milk out of me."

Mrs Bunnet frowned at her daughter. Despite her best attempts at inculcating the manners of the aristocracy at home, there was only so much one could do. Her younger daughters had not had the benefit of exposure to polite London society of their older siblings. Their formative years had been almost entirely in Niddry and Craigmillar, and their language was often forthright.

"What?" said Lydia, glaring back at her mother. "I'm thirsty!"

"It takes four litres of water to make a litre of milk," said Mary. "I saw a video about it on YouTube when I was in the library."

Mr McCallister deflected the tension by sending Ross to fetch five pint glasses of tap water from the kitchen. They were actually half litre glasses, pint glasses having been banned by the EU many years before, but Mr McCallister was fighting a personal rearguard action to preserve imperial measures.

"I only recently moved in," he explained. "My patron, Lady Catherine Bampot, has placed the manse at my disposal. She feels that as the leader of the Tory party, I should have a representative dwelling close to the parliament building. The Manse will be a stepping stone to Bute House."

"It is very pleasant," said Mrs Bunnet, "and most generous of Lady Catherine."

"Indeed, it is," he replied. "She is, of course, fantastically wealthy and a great friend of the party."

"And to what do we owe the honour of this invitation?" asked Mrs Bunnet.

"Lady Catherine believes that as a potential future First Minister it is essential for me to acquire a wife. And she suggested that of all the debutantes, I should pay especial attention to your charming daughters."

"I am sure my daughters are honoured by Lady Catherine's approbation. Although, I do not think I have ever met the lady."

"Her ladyship moves in rarified circles. But she became aware of the... special circumstances... surrounding your daughters and passed the information on to me. So perhaps we should start there: can you confirm that the rumours which reached Lady Catherine are true? That your daughters have a licence to bear children?"

"That is true. My daughters each have a licence from the government of Italy to bear a single child. Their MedChips were installed in Italy and their fertility is not under the control of the Scottish Government."

"Then it is settled. And Mrs Bunnet, I assure you that when the Pàrtaidh Tòraidheach na h-Alba comes to power, one of my first priorities will be to create a second chamber for the Scottish Parliament. You can expect a seat in the Scottish House of Lords and your allowances and expenses will be restored."

"And my former title?"

"Of course, my government will ensure the Lord Lyon's disgraceful decision on pre-independence titles is reversed. I assume that, if restored to a Scottish House of Lords, you would sit as a Tory?"

"You can trust me to follow the party line on every vote when I'm present in parliament."

"Oh, there will be no need to be present. When we restore the Lords, we will have electronic voting. It'll just be a matter of handing your password over to my assistant and we will handle everything. There will be no need for a debating chamber, we will set the Lords up as a members' club with an excellent restaurant and discreet guest bedrooms somewhere in the New Town."

"Even better," said Mrs Bunnet.

Mr McAllister nodded. "Then, in that case, all that remains is to decide on which of your beautiful daughters I should bestow my favour."

"I'm sure any one of them would be honoured, sir. Say hello to Mr McCallister, girls. You start Jane, you're the eldest."

"Jane may be the eldest," grumbled Lydia, "but I'm the tallest, it's not fair, she's always first!"

"Would you mind standing up?" asked Mr McCallister, "and perhaps turn around so I can get a good look at each of you."

After the visit concluded, Mrs Bunnet considered it had gone well. To be sure, Mr McAllister was more than twice the age of her daughters and not as wealthy as she could have hoped for, but a possible future First Minister was not a catch to be sneezed at. After all, she had five daughters and it was unrealistic to expect they would all find a billionaire.

— ♦ —

After their meeting with Mr McCallister, the Bunnets left the manse and walked the short distance down the Canongate along the side of the parliament towards Holyrood Palace.

"Oh God, it's Mad Nadz," said Mrs Bunnet as they arrived at the paved plaza at the front of the parliament. "Don't look, keep going girls. Maybe she won't see us."

Mad Nadz McNevin was the Bunnet's lodger, she was wearing her favourite peasant dress and standing on the low concrete wall which surrounded the decorative pool outside the parliament. She looked unsteady, like she might fall in and she was ranting something at the passing tourists. Two police officers, posted outside the parliament with assault rifles cradled across their chests, stood a few metres away making no attempt to intervene. There was nothing they could do, because Nadz was an elected Member of the Scottish Parliament - albeit on the list. Normally Nadz haunted a shaded concrete bench in a secluded area between the parliament and Dynamic Earth where she could drink and doze undisturbed. Today, however, Nadz had stationed herself outside the parliament as a warmup for an appearance in the chamber in her role as Shadow Culture Secretary.

Mad Nadz, finished her diatribe, took a half-bottle from her bag and had a quick gulp and then looked around for a new victim. Unfortunately for the Bunnets, their route from the Royal Mile to the pelican crossing at Horse Wynd took them past Nadz just as she looked up.

Nadz focussed on Lizzie and stepped carefully off the low wall. Despite her caution, her execution of the manouevre was imperfect; she lost her balance and toppled forward two steps before recovering. Her face was close enough to Lizzie's that Lizzie could smell gin.

"Welcome to Holyrood!" declaimed Mad Nadz. Unlike the tourists, Lizzie had heard it before.

"Go Nadz!" mocked Lydia. Mrs Bunnet scowled.

"Welcome to Holyrood!" Nadz repeated, somewhat louder, taking Lydia's comment as encouragement and waving her bottle to indicate the parliament, "Everyone comes to Holyrood, got a dream!" Nadz paused for a drop of refreshment before delivering the punchline. "What's your dream?!" She fixed Elizabeth with her gaze and repeated, "What's your dream, Lizzie Bunnet?"

Her work completed, Ms McNevin stumbled back to her previous station on the low wall surrounding the pool and scouted for her next victim while the Bunnets continued on their way. They entered through the palace gift shop and made a brief detour into the customer toilets to reconfigure their attire, restoring the more bulky elements of the wedding dress and donning the matching millinery. Their invitations were checked, and they passed through a metal detector before emerging into the courtyard. A small queue of debutantes had formed in front of the palace entrance, waiting for the door to be opened. It reminded Mrs Bunnet of the queue for the City Farm, except that instead of the green farm uniform the debutantes were wearing white dresses, veils and hats with swan plumes and their mothers were decked out in extravagant hats and designer dresses and dripping with jewellery. Mrs Bunnet's dress was at least as costly as those of her counterparts, but her hips had expanded substantially since the glory days of her youth and her dress had not. The consequence of more material being required to cover her posterior was less material being available to cover her legs, and the hemline had risen several inches above the level which the designer had intended. At eleven a.m. on the dot, the front door of the palace opened, and a footman directed the gentlefolk to the King's drawing room. The presentation was less daunting than that in the English court; the King was sitting on one of his smaller thrones and attended by only a few senior courtiers, a small team of servants, and a quartet of musicians to provide a pleasant acoustic ambience. After a few minutes, it was the Bunnets' turn.

"Her Grace the Cuntess of Craigmillar accompanied by her daughters." announced the footman as they entered the room. This was the moment Mrs Bunnet had been dreading, but at least there were fewer people than she had expected to witness her disgrace. After independence the Scottish Government had considered rescinding all life peerages conferred by English Prime Ministers for political reasons but, after consultation with the Lord Lyon King of Arms, had decided that, as a compromise, the title of life peers should be changed from Baron and Baroness to Count and Countess with the option to use the Scottish spelling.

Mrs Bunnet approached the King and curtseyed. By some miracle, the fabric of her dress held out against the strain despite being several sizes too small. Orders and decorations were worn when attending court and she had three medals pinned to the front of her frock. The first was the badge of the Most Dishonourable Order of Judas Iscariot: a simple lead disk bearing the image of a hanged man suspended above thirty pieces of silver and the words 'Traitor Knave'. It was a requirement that any aristocrat whose title was received from the English as a bribe for opposing independence wore this medal when attending court functions. The second, a simple bronze disk, was a long service medal from the Brothel, and the third was a Best In Show award from the Royal Highland Society for Cheddar cheese.

"Welcome, Countess Bunnet," said His Majesty, graciously opting not to use the abbreviated form of her title. "It is many years since we have seen you at court. And these are your lovely daughters?"

"Yes, Your Majesty. May I introduce Jane, my eldest?"

Jane came forward and made a low curtsey. The King held out his hand, and she kissed his ring.

"The very best of luck to you," said the King, "I am sure you will make an excellent match and look forward to seeing you at court again."

Jane thanked His Majesty and carefully backed away from the throne. She'd been instructed that it was against court etiquette to turn your back on the King. The King himself rather regretted missing out on a rear view of the debutantes and was seriously considering repealing this rule.

Everything passed without incident until it was Lydia's turn. After being introduced to twenty debutantes, the King was getting bored.

"May the matrimonial odds be ever in your favour!" he said, instead of the standard greeting.

The change from rehearsals disconcerted Lydia. She made a particularly low curtsey and, as she rose, her heel caught on the train of her frock. Instead of moving back into the curtsey and allowing her mother to unhook the errant shoe, she flexed her muscles and tried to overcome the resistance.

Unfortunately, the Brothel issue wedding dress was held together with velcro in strategic locations. There was a ripping sound and the entire skirt and train fell to the floor around Lydia's ankles, leaving her in the white stockings, suspenders and crotchless lace panties of the Brothel's 'bride' outfit.

"Oops," said Lydia, not at all embarrassed by her situation, and bent down to retrieve the lower part of her dress.

"No doubt, I shall see you again," said the King with a wink and turned to his equerry, Sir Philip McCann.

"Make a note Sir Philip. I've got dibs if this one ends up in the Brothel."

"Fat chance of Lydia Bunnet not ending up in the Brothel!" snorted the equerry. "Her name's been down ever since she was born."

— ♦ —

The Bunnet family made their exit and returned to the palace cafe beside the gift shop. Mrs Bunnet took a table with a view over the courtyard and observed the debutantes coming and going while her daughters made use of the cafe toilets to reconfigure their clothing. When they emerged, the long trains were gone and stuffed into the carrier bags, the skirts were shorter than before and their hats had been put away. Considerably less impeded by superfluous fabric, the young ladies and their mother left the palace.

On the previous evening Mrs Bunnet had enquired of her husband as to whether the van was required and, on being informed that it was not, had requested its use for their return journey. Accordingly, they made their way round the side of the palace and into the park where they were greeted by the familiar and joyous jingle emitted by the family ice-cream van. Space in the back of the vintage van was limited and there were no seats, but the five daughters had developed a system which allowed them to squeeze in and duck low enough not to be seen. Their mother sat up front in the passenger seat and their father drove.

"My dear Mr Bunnet," said his lady to him, "have you heard of the yacht which berthed in the Forth yesterday?"

Mr Bunnet replied that he had not.

"Justice Cockburn says Baron Bampot's four mast steam cruiser is completely in its shade."

Mr Bunnet made no reply.

"Do you not want to know who's yacht it is?" said his wife impatiently.

"You want to tell me, and I have no objection to hearing it."

"Justice Cockburn says it is owned by Mr Arseny Parslikov, a Russian businessman."

Mr Bunnet took his eyes off the road to face her.

"Arseny Parslikov," he said, "that's the Russian oligarch that's trying to buy Hearts. Isn't it?"

Mrs Bunnet replied that she did not know, but that it was a fine thing for their girls.

"How so?"

"My dear Mr Bunnet," replied his wife, "how can you be so tiresome! You know that they are to be married this season."

"Is it your design that one of the girls marries this oligarch?"

"Design! Nonsense, how can you talk so? But when Mr Parslikov learns that our daughters are the only ladies in Scotland who are fertile, it is likely that he may be interested in one of them. And who is to know what will happen then?"

Mr Bunnet's property consisted almost entirely of a two-story house on the Craigmillar Estate. To be more accurate, the property actually belonged to Edinburgh City Council and was, in fact, the last council house in Scotland. Mr Bunnet had acquired the tenancy many years before, thanks to his Masonic connections in the Labour Party. The rent was affordable and had not been raised since they moved in. However, despite the upgrade from the original stained grey pebble dash to a pastel shade of blue, the property was far from photogenic and their neighbours in the private new-build houses that surrounded it considered it an eyesore. The house had a small front garden which the Bunnet's had successfully re-wilded over the course of their tenancy, but the back garden was paved over. One side of it was used as a parking space for the van and the other was taken up by a rusted shipping container which functioned as Mr Bunnet's shed.

It was a desirable residence despite its aesthetic deficiencies: the accommodation was at least ten times the size of what a private landlord would provide for the same rent. The only drawback was that the tenancy was entailed and on the death of the sitting tenant, Mr Bunnet, the council would be able to offer it to someone with more recent political connections. There was no doubt in Mrs Bunnet's mind they would waste no time in evicting the family, and most likely seek to recoup the substantial rent arrears as well.

The Bunnet house was at the far end of the housing scheme on the edge of the countryside. Rather than use a mere number which might give away that it was a terraced house, the Bunnets had named their property 'Jambourn'. The name was a compromise reflecting Mrs Bunnet's love of Jane Austen novels and Mr Bunnet's devotion to Heart Of Midlothian FC. A hundred metres further up Craigmillar Castle Road, at the top of the hill, were the ruins of the eponymous Craigmillar Castle. Mr Bunnet turned into a lane which ran between school playing fields and the rear of the house and provided access to their back garden.

The Bunnets entered through the back door and made their way through the kitchen to the living room. A motorised armchair which Mr Bunnet had purchased on e-Bay had pride of place in the room. Primary attraction of the chair was that, should the necessity arise to stand up, it could assist the process by raising and angling the seat. The occasion seldom arose, however, for Mr Bunnet had a large supply of incontinence pants conveniently pre-positioned next to his chair along with a two litre bottle of Tesco's finest cider and his daily ration of Fuel. A second notable fixture was the Royal Warrant installed above the fireplace. The warrant was a metre high, hand carved from solid oak and professionally gilded. It had once adorned the reception area of Mrs Bunnet's underwear business and had been surreptitiously removed before the administrators auctioned off the assets. It now made an impressive if somewhat overpowering addition to the Bunnet's small living room. Pride swelled in Mrs Bunnet's breast every time she regarded the Royal Crest and the inscription under it, "By Appointment to His Majesty's Brothel, Bunnet International Ltd., Purveyors of Crotchless Panties."

It was these panties which had propelled Mrs Bunnet's business on its meteoric rise to fortune. After her previous employer decided her services were no longer required, Miss Bunnet, as she was then, had taken temporary employment with the Brothel. Inspiration struck after she mislaid three pairs of underpants in one week. It was simply too easy to forget to collect them after her duties were concluded.

Moreover, precious time was wasted removing them only to put them back on. What was needed was crotchless panties, comfortable but made of fabric strong enough to withstand the rigours of the workplace. After many abortive experiments, she eventually found a textile developed by the US Department of Defense as ballistic protection underwear for commandos. The rest was lingerie history.

— ♦ —

The last of the debutantes kissed the King's ring just after one o'clock and with a sigh of relief, he got off the throne and stretched.

"What else have we got on today?" he asked his equerry.

"The First Minister's monthly audience is at two o'clock, Your Majesty. And there are birthday cards to sign."

The King sighed. "We should've put the age for the birthday card up, Sir Philip. Just about everybody lives to a hundred these days."

"I agree Sire, but with the Government thinking about abolishing the monarchy, we can't afford to offend the pensioners."

"I suppose you're right. Anyway, I should get on. I need to change out of these ridiculous court clothes and have lunch before the First Minister gets here."

The meetings with the First Minister were a monthly highlight for the King. She always had interesting news and she was forthright and down to earth. When they were alone, she didn't fawn over him like everybody else. She also had very similar views on the monarchy to his own: it was a ridiculous anachronism which should be abolished at some unspecified future date - but not yet. Since there were no photographs planned, the King decided not to bother with a suit and instead changed into casual clothes from a high-end outdoor clothing brand. Hill walking had been his passion in younger years and although he got little chance to do it these days, he still liked to dress the part, even if it was only for a walk in Holyrood Park. The King knew the park like the back of his hand. He used the side paths on the less frequented hills on either side of Arthur's Seat and he liked to walk at dusk, when there were fewer people and more wildlife.

The First Minister had come across from the parliament and was wearing her trademark blue dress. The equerry showed her to the King's private office; the King greeted his guest, and the equerry left them alone. His Majesty then locked the door from the inside. This was protocol, because they might be discussing classified information. The entire wall of the King's study behind his desk was occupied by a floor to ceiling bookcase. The First Minister looked away as the King removed a volume two sections from the left and three shelves up, and pressed a hidden catch. A section of the bookcase detached from the rest and, with a little effort, the King pulled it out and swung it open on cunningly designed hinges. Taking their coffee and biscuits with them, they adjourned to the truly private section of the King's private office.

None of the staff knew about this room and the King was not much for housework, so it was dusty and untidy. The secret area was not an original feature of the palace, it had been constructed by a specialist military contractor to serve as a panic room for the King should the palace be attacked. There was no window. Three of the walls were thick stone outer walls of the palace, the fourth was an inch thick steel plate behind the bookcase. Ventilation was from a military system intended for nuclear bunkers.

"This is new," said the First Minister and walked across to admire an ancient tapestry which the King had attached to the steel panel behind the bookcase using strips of duct tape.

"I found it in storage in the Royal Collection," said the King, "it's the family tree of the four wealthiest noble families in Scotland."

The First Minister nodded. The top section of the tapestry was obviously a family tree for four families, the Campbells, Murrays, Mintos, and Seuchars. Centuries of marriages and births were recorded in an orderly fashion, with occasional cross links between the families until, at a point near the bottom of the tapestry, the neat structure exploded into a tangled mess. From that point on, instead of neat embroidery, there was a forest of PostIt notes and pieces of string.

"What on earth happened to the tapestry?" asked the First Minister.

"The Scottish Government legalised polygamy and passed the Gender Identification Act," replied the King. "A few years later, the seamstress who had been extending it each year had a minor nervous breakdown and resigned. I updated the bottom section myself."

The First Minister laughed, "Well, that's a side effect we didn't think about when we passed those laws."

"Something else happened," said the King, "don't you see it?"

"I just see a rat's nest of string and sticky notes."

"The family trees of the Mintos, Murrays and Seuchars stopped growing," said the King. "They stopped moving downwards. The last few years, they have just been adding more and more connections at the same level."

"What do you mean?"

"I mean that none of these families, apart from the Campbells, have had a child born since 2028. The Campbells have a single child born to the illegitimate daughter of the former owner of this Palace."

"Surely that's not a surprise, since the UN Population Control Treaty almost no licences to have children are issued."

"Perhaps. But these families are more than wealthy enough to purchase a licence and they have done so on several occasions. But not a single one has resulted in a child."

"That is certainly curious."

"It is more than curious. These four families own ninety percent of the rural land in Scotland. The Campbells also own many properties in the cities. As you know, wealth has become more and more concentrated. It was happening before independence and it has happened even faster since. But there is no next generation to inherit it."

"We need to tax land or wealth," said the First Minister, "I've always thought it was the right thing, but it's too difficult. The electoral system was set up before independence to prevent majority governments. It has its advantages, but it makes radical reforms almost impossible. Wealth taxes would face total opposition not only from the rich but from the upper middle classes and young people who believe they are going to be rich. The media is controlled by the rich. If we put wealth or land taxes in our manifesto, we would lose the election. It's been that way for twenty-five years."

"I completely agree," said the King. "Wealth taxes are both essential to counteract the concentration of wealth and politically impossible because the rich, and those who think they will become rich, have too much power. But I think somebody else may be dealing with the situation for you."

"I don't follow. How can anyone else reform the tax system?"

"There hasn't been a birth in these families since 2028, which means there were no pregnancies since 2027," said the King, "do you remember what happened in 2027?"

"2027 was a few years after independence. Things were quite wild at that time. There was the problem with Mr McLeod."

"The Land Reform Minister in the first SNP government after independence, Professor Harmatia McTavish, died in a motorcycle accident in 2027."

"Yes, I remember. She was making some progress on land reform, but I don't see the relevance."

"Professor McTavish was the co-founder of MedChip corporation, along with Dr Knox. Which, I would surmise given the advanced technology involved in the MedChips, would mean she was also a senior member of the Guild. The rumour at the time was that someone had tampered with the brakes on her motorcycle."

"The birth control laws are enforced by MedChips. So your theory is the Guild is taking revenge on the landowning families because they think they murdered Professor McTavish?"

"Possibly it is revenge, possibly whoever is doing this just wishes to carry out Professor McTavish's land reform agenda. If these families cannot have children, there will be no heirs to their property. They can hang on for a while by marrying younger spouses, but eventually someone will die without an heir and their property will fall to the state. It is a slow but certain method of breaking up their landholdings."

"This is the Guild we are talking about," said the First Minister, "they don't always stay dead. It could even be Professor McTavish herself, uploaded onto a computer or resurrected in some other way."

"It could indeed," said the King, "but the relevant point is that the problem may take care of itself if you are patient. There's no need to rush in with unpopular legislation that might lose you the election."

"You mean the consultation on aristocratic titles and the monarchy?"

"Exactly. Powerful people like judges and senior academics and civil servants have been looking forward to receiving a knighthood or peerage. They like dressing up and coming to garden parties and dream that their family will also become landed gentry and live off rents in a country house for generations. You are turning the establishment against your government."

"Surely, with all the land tied up by four families, it's even less likely that newcomers aspiring to become landowners will be able to achieve their goal?"

"Logically, splitting up the landholdings would actually make it easier for newcomers to acquire an estate. But it isn't the way they are thinking. They will help the aristocrats preserve their wealth forever, because they hope some day to retain wealth in their family forever."

"I've tried to make the case that it is the wrong time to move on this inside the party. The problem is we've been in power for twenty-five years and we've not done anything about the monarchy, the aristocracy or land reform. Patience has run out. If I don't do anything, they will find another leader. The consultation on aristocratic titles and the monarchy is the smallest step which the party would accept."

"This isn't the time, First Minister, the monarchy is popular, and the aristocracy is powerful: pushing too hard and letting the Tories in would be a step backward."

"I don't disagree with any of that, but my hands are tied."

The King sensed the topic was becoming uncomfortable for his guest and continuing with it would be impolite. It was time to draw a halt to the business element of their meeting.

"Seeing as we are in the most secure room of the palace, perhaps I could interest you in a very special tipple, First Minister?"

He opened an ornate drinks cabinet and took out a black glass bottle and two small crystal glasses. There was no label on the bottle.

"Is that what I think it is?" asked the First Minister, "I've been briefed about it, but I've never actually seen it."

The King pulled the cork out of the bottle and held it out so she could smell the aroma.

"Morningside Mist," he said, "I managed to acquire a bottle."

The First Minister gasped.

"Do you realise how illegal that stuff is?" she asked. "It breaks the EU directive on whisky purity, the UN treaty banning animal dairy products and an intergovernmental agreement with Ireland."

The King smiled and tapped his nose with his finger. "I won't tell if you don't. And nobody else ever comes into this room."

He poured a measure from the bottle into each of the two glasses. It was a thick, creamy brown liquid with a delightful aroma somewhere between coffee and whisky.

They sat back on the King's comfortable armchairs and chatted while taking tiny sips of the costly liqueur and savouring every drop.

Sunshiners

Around about the same time as the Bunnets arrived home, Justice Elaine Cockburn packed up her books in the Signet Library after a morning spent researching arcane historical laws and precedents. The research wasn't part of her normal duties: Justice Cockburn was a member of the Most Noble Order of the Garter Belt and, as a privy councillor, was occasionally asked to advise His Majesty on legal matters. Elaine was normally an avid royalist, but she was currently sulking about not getting the baronetcy she had expected and not feeling particularly motivated. Moreover, it was Friday and knocking off early was a tradition for the Edinburgh legal establishment. But the key factor was that Sheriff Bellenden's temporary wife Madame l'Hôpital had introduced her to a new hobby, and she couldn't wait to get home.

Cheesemaking had replaced baking as the obsession of the upper classes. Ever since the United Nations had banned farming animals in order to mitigate carbon emissions, cow, sheep and goat's milk were not legally available. There were artificial substitutes, but the law stated that they needed to be marked as such prominently on the packaging and it was generally accepted that the taste was inferior to natural milk. Whether it tasted worse was arguable, but it certainly tasted different because it was also illegal for a manufacturer of artificial milk to make it taste like the natural product. The reason for these regulations was economic: the government derived a substantial fraction of its revenue from the penal system and one of the principal revenue generators was the sale of human milk and semen.

Mrs Bunnet's attendance at the milking parlour was compulsory, her milk was sold to make payments towards a debt she had incurred as the result of a large fine. However, her daughters and Elaine were there voluntarily. Elaine was collecting milk for her cheesemaking hobby and the Bunnet daughters were contributing to the family ice cream business. As an amateur producing cheese for private consumption, it would have been perfectly legal for Elaine to collect her milk at home, but she preferred to have the farm pasteurise the milk and document the source and date of production. Elaine loved paperwork, rules, and regulations and, to avoid the slightest suspicion that she might be using illegally sourced milk, she'd registered as a cheese manufacturer and was following all the rules for commercial cheese production. That meant the provenance of every drop of milk needed to be recorded as well as the weight of every block of cheese produced.

The kitchen of Elaine's house had been transformed for her cheesemaking project, and she had enlisted the services of family and friends. Elaine's wife Justine had borrowed equipment from her aunt's farm and all available surfaces in the kitchen were covered in metal bowls, mixers, chillers and laboratory equipment whose purpose Elaine could not fathom. As well as Madame l'Hôpital, who was acting as a consultant, and Justine, Elaine's daughter Hestia, was also present via a video call from the Guild's space station. Hestia was sitting at a desk in a small student-dorm like room. Mars was visible through a window on her right, silhouetted against the blackness of space. Behind her, Elaine could see a set of shelves with a few antique paper books, a picture of the family and the cup she'd been presented with at the prize-giving ceremony at the Guild's school. Elaine didn't realise it, but Hestia's window was not a real window but a computer screen simulating one. It was more practical to keep the outer surface of the space station free of unnecessary openings and, in any case, since the station was rotating to maintain artificial gravity, the view from a real window would be nausea inducing.

"Hello mum!" said Hestia, "have you brought it?"

Elaine took the precious flask from her bag and held it up for Hestia to see.

"Just over a litre!"

"That will take us above 10 litres in total. We have enough to start the process, but we can't afford any spills or mistakes!"

"Au travail!" said Madame l'Hôpital, placing her iPad on the table so they could consult the recipe. "The first thing is to mix the milk together. Justine, can you sniff the bottles before we mix them in? If one has gone off, the whole batch would be ruined."

"They won't have gone off," said Elaine. "They were pasteurised at the City Farm before I collected them, and they've been in the fridge ever since."

"It only takes a second to check," replied Madame l'Hôpital, "and if something is wrong, it's better to discover it immediately and throw away one litre of milk now, rather than throw away the whole block of cheese in a few weeks."

Justine unscrewed the lid on the new bottle and sniffed carefully. A few years before, as a result of a Guild science experiment, she had had sections of Labrador and cat DNA inserted into her genome. Technically, she was now a human, Labrador, cat, chimaera or, as she preferred to say, were-Labracat. As a consequence, she had acquired a preternaturally acute sense of smell.

"Human milk," she said, "medium fat, very slight note of single malt whisky. Glencarbost I believe. Did you have a dram last night?"

"Just a small one," said Elaine.

"I doubt a human will be able to taste it," said Justine, "but we agreed you wouldn't drink while we were collecting milk for our project."

"It'll be fine," said Elaine. "Besides, whisky has less of a kick than it used to. Chocolate biscuits are the same. I need to have two with my coffee when before one was enough."

"You should cut down mum, alcohol and sugar aren't good for you," said Hestia, "it sounds like your body has developed a tolerance."

"Maybe I should cut down," said Elaine. "But I'm sure they are making the biscuits smaller and I think the whisky isn't as strong either."

"Too late now!" said Madame l'Hôpital, "In any case a drop of whisky will improve the flavour." She placed the bottle on a laboratory balance, noted the weight, and then tipped the precious fluid into a large, flat-bottomed flask. One by one, nine more bottles were taken from the fridge, checked by Justine and added to the flask.

Madame l'Hôpital read from the instructions on the iPad.

"According to the original recipe, we need to add Calcium Chloride and stir for one minute."

"How much milk do we have?" asked Hestia.

"10,273 grammes," said Justine.

"Then we need to add an eighth of a mole," said Hestia.

Elaine was shocked. "That's disgusting! And anyway, where on earth am I supposed to get moles in Edinburgh on a Friday afternoon?"

Hestia sighed.

"Just put in 13.9 grammes of Calcium Chloride, mum," she said, "then put the flask on the automated stirrer at 0.55 revolutions per second and set the timer for 63 seconds. Justine, do you have the bacteria ready?"

"Yes," said Justine, "I downloaded the data you provided into the DNA synthesiser in my aunt's laboratory and inserted the synthetic DNA into a sample Penicillium Roqueforti bacteria using CRISPR, 0.5 grammes of the novel bacteria was cultured from the sample with the engineered DNA inserted and I've prepared it in solution to use."

"Does it smell right?"

Justine needed to sniff the sample several times. Finally, she replied.

"At first I thought it was exactly the same as the mold in Blue Lanark cheese, but actually there is a very subtle difference."

"Probably you can smell the genetic alterations to the mold bacteria to optimise it for human milk." said Hestia. "Your Labrador nose is impressive. Hopefully, the palette of the judges is less so!"

Madame l'Hôpital snorted.

"There is no doubt about that, in France with a professional Chef de Fromage, it would be different. Here in Scotland, the judges at your Highland Show will notice nothing!"

The stirring machine made a 'ting' sound and stopped.

"Now we add 0.48 millilitres of the mold solution," said Hestia, "Set the temperature to 31.1 centigrade and then we have to give the bacteria 89 minutes and 23 seconds to act on the milk before the next step."

"This is a kitchen, not a science lab!" complained Madame l'Hôpital. "There should be creativity and passion!"

"I'm a scientist, not a chef," said Hestia. "But I've double checked all the simulations and I'm confident if we follow the process exactly it will result in a product which is chemically as close as is possible to Blue Lanark cheese when one starts from human milk. Unfortunately, even the Guild's computers cannot predict the subjective taste. But if the chemical composition is nearly the same, it should taste nearly the same."

"The proof of the pudding is in the eating! And also the proof of the cheese," said Madame l'Hôpital, "and that is why the palate of a French woman is indispensable!"

Elaine agreed. She had appointed Madame l'Hôpital as an honorary consultant to her cheese making team purely on the basis of her French citizenship. With Madame l'Hôpital's palate and Justine's Labracat nose, Hestia's genetic engineering skills, the use of at least half a billion euros worth of Guild lab equipment and supercomputers along with the excellent raw material she produced herself there was no question their cheese would be best in its category at the Royal Highland Show. Elaine allowed herself to daydream of next month's royal garden party, where, even if she did not have the baroness title she deserved, she could hold her head up high with a gold medal from the Royal Highland Show pinned to her dress.

— ♦ —

"Right mum," said Hestia, "now we've finished with the cheesemaking, let's check your whisky."

"What?"

"Go and get your whisky. I'm worried about you. You say the whisky is weaker than it used to be. I think you may be drinking too much and developing a tolerance. We can easily see who is right by measuring the alcohol content with the lab equipment we brought for the cheesemaking. If it's what it's supposed to be, I want you to promise to cut back."

Elaine didn't like being preached to by her daughter, but she was curious to have the whisky measured because it really did feel like it was having less effect.

She came back with her bottle of 10-year-old Glencarbost.

"Don't take too much, though. It's expensive!"

"Don't worry, mum. We just need to collect 100ml and weigh it. We'll put it back afterwards. Justine, do you know how to do it?"

"Miaow!" said Justine. Her aunt, Dr Dickson, was excited by the scientific potential of combining the sensitivity of Justine's Labrador nose with a knowledge of organic chemistry and had encouraged her to sit in on some classes from the Guild school and learn how to use laboratory equipment. Justine was proud of her new skills and eager to show them off, especially since she suspected that people were taking her less seriously since she had acquired the cat and dog genes. It was true that she now liked to chase balls and have her belly rubbed and sometimes said 'miaow' or 'woof' instead of yes or no, but she was every bit as intelligent as before.

She started by weighing the 100ml measuring cylinder, then she filled it with 100ml of distilled water and weighed it again. Finally she weighed it with 100ml of whisky.

"Ambient temperature is 21.5 centigrade, the measurements should be made at 20 centigrade but it is close enough. The measuring cylinder weighs 19.2 grammes. With 100ml of distilled water, it weighs 118.9 grammes. With 100ml of Elaine's whisky, it weighs 110.8 grammes."

"OK, that sounds about right. The whisky is a little lighter because alcohol is less dense than water. What's the alcohol by volume supposed to be, it should say, on the bottle?"

Elaine examined the label.

"It says 45.8% ABV. Is that alcohol by volume?"

"Yep, that's what I need. Hold on till I do the sums."

There was a long pause.

"Are you sure you did all the measurements carefully, Justine? You measured the volumes from the bottom of the meniscus?" asked Hestia.

"Miaow!" said Justine angrily. "My aunt wouldn't have trusted me with her equipment if I didn't know what I was doing."

"I'm sorry, you're right. If Dr Dickson trusts you, that's good enough for me. It's just that if the measurements are correct, then Mum's whisky really has been watered down. If it was 45.8% proof, the whisky sample would have weighed 109.4 grammes. It is almost a gramme and a half too heavy, which means more water and less alcohol."

"Sacrebleue!" exclaimed Madame l'Hôpital.

— ♦ —

At that moment, the house computer announced that Madame l'Hôpital's temporary husband Roger Bellenden was at the front door. He was an old friend of the family and the facial recognition identified him before he had time to press the doorbell.

"Computer, open the front door!" said Elaine.

A few minutes later, he joined them in the kitchen. Friday was wife swapping day and Roger had come to collect Justine.

"All finished with the cheesemaking?" he asked. "Ready to go, Justine?"

"Sure, I just need to put some clothes on. I won't be a minute." Justine didn't bother with clothes at home because she had fur.

"What's the whisky for?" asked Roger, "you're not putting it in the cheese are you?"

"We just measured the alcohol content," said Elaine. "I thought it was getting weaker and everybody else thought I was imagining it, but it turns out I was right and it had been watered down."

"You're kidding!" said Roger.

"No," said Hestia, "the most likely explanation for the measured alcohol by volume compared with the value stated on the label is that someone removed 100ml of whisky from the 700ml bottle and replaced it with water."

Roger held the bottle up to the light.

"The colour looks about right," he said sceptically. "If somebody had watered it down, wouldn't it be a lighter shade?"

"Let me smell it," said Justine.

She sniffed. This time, it didn't take long to reach a conclusion.

"Glencarbost, 10-year-old. But I also smell food colourant E155."

"E155 is brown," said Hestia. "This is a professional job. They are trying to match the colour of the original whisky by adding food dye to the water they use to dilute it. A human would almost certainly be fooled."

Roger frowned, then he turned to Elaine.

"I wonder if this might be something for us."

"I don't see how, surely weights and measures fraud is something for Europol or Police Scotland Recent Crimes Division."

"Hear me out," said Roger. "Our department handles historic crimes and grievances."

"Yes, but this is a recent crime."

"That is a matter of interpretation. 'Historic crimes' could mean crimes committed a long time ago. But it could also mean crimes under historic laws which have fallen into disuse."

"It's a stretch, but possibly arguable."

"The thing is," said Roger, "there are some absolute crackers of historic laws about watering down whisky. The idea of prosecuting statues for historic crimes was good for a couple of seasons, but audience numbers are falling again. Blowing up a statue doesn't have the same impact as sentencing a live defendant."

Cases at the Historic Crimes and Grievances Court were always accompanied by a TV documentary outlining the prosecution case and, as the season finale, live coverage of the trial and punishment of the offender.

"Watering down whisky will certainly get a powerful reaction from our viewers. Are you thinking about next year's series?"

"I was thinking perhaps a Hogmanay Special. If we can get some extra TV revenue, it could keep us safe from the next round of cuts. Did you hear they finally axed the police mounted section? The Justice Secretary instructed the Chief Constable to put the horses and equipment into the auction at the Highland Show."

"As long as we are making a profit, they won't touch us," said Elaine, "and a Hogmanay Special would make sure we hit our numbers."

"Hold on," said Justine, "doing an extra show may be a good idea for your department, but so far you've only found one bottle of watered down whisky. It's not much of a crime unless you can establish it is happening on a large scale."

"You're right," said Roger. "As officers of the court, it is our duty to check a lot more samples. I wonder if we can put them on expenses."

— ♦ —

Usually, on the Saturday morning after a wife-swapping Friday, Justine woke in Sheriff Bellenden's 1000 thread count Egyptian cotton sheets. Today, she didn't even have her basket; she was curled up in a ball on an old sofa. Her fur was tangled and matted, her mouth was dry, and she had a headache. At least the headache had temporarily taken care of her sexual frustration. Somewhere nearby, she could hear Madame l'Hôpital in conversation with her friend Victoria.

"Ooh-la-la," said Madame l'Hôpital, "Justine's husband, Jeffrey, he is a big one."

This comment did not help Justine's mood. When Jeffrey, had registered a female identity, Elaine, in order to apply for a promotion to the Supreme Court which was only open to women, she'd assumed that he'd still use his male identity at home, but for the last few months he'd only done so on Friday nights when Madame l'Hôpital was visiting.

"But," continued Madame l'Hôpital, "in my opinion, one should not differentiate based on the distance…"

"… but the velocity. That is my rule. Jeffrey, he has the length but Roger, he has the speed and they are equally effective."

"It's an interesting theory," said Victoria, "but that is only two data points. What about your husband in France?"

"My husband in France, he drinks too much. When there is a problem with the dt's, it is not possible to differentiate," replied Madame l'Hôpital.

Justine raised her head and forced her eyes open. She was in the cafe in the arcade in South Bridge. The sun was already up, but the cafe wasn't open. Her friend Claire was lying on the floor a little to her left, covered with a coat and with a cushion from one of the sofas for a pillow. Claire's husband David was sitting slumped forward over a table with his head on his hands. Sheriff Bellenden and Elaine were lying together on the other sofa.

With a start, Justine sprang to her feet. Elaine and Victoria were here with her, but the kids were not!

"Who's watching the kids?" she yelled.

Elaine groaned and opened one eye.

"Don't worry, they are at home with Frances. Go back to sleep."

But Justine was awake now. She walked unsteadily over and joined Victoria and Madame l'Hôpital at their table.

"What happened?" she asked.

"Gathering evidence," said Madame l'Hôpital, and touched the side of her nose conspiratorially with one finger. But suddenly her eyes felt heavy and her head started to pound and she decided to rest it on the table for a while.

"Claire and Victoria wanted to help, so we decided to use the arcade as our base because there's lots of pubs and off-licences nearby," said Elaine.

"How much did I drink?"

"Hard to say," said Victoria. "You were full on Labrador last night and there was a lot of whisky about. At first you were just sniffing it, but after a while your tongue was coming out."

In order to use her Labrador sense of smell to best effect, Justine had to channel the Labrador side of her personality. There was no way the Labrador would sniff whisky samples for hours without trying any.

"OK, is there a bathroom here? I need to clean my fur and sober up. Possibly I need to puke."

"Downstairs," said Victoria. "Watch out, though. James is down there in the office, either sleeping or playing TDA."

"Mruggh," said Justine. She was too hungover to miaow properly.

Claire was the next to wake. She went behind the bar to make coffee, and the sound of the coffee machine woke everyone else.

"It's 2047," complained Claire. "You'd think they could make MedChips that took care of hangovers!"

"They used to," said David, "when the MedChips first came out. But they changed them because it resulted in people drinking too much. I wouldn't be surprised if the newest ones even make hangover symptoms worse. They're supposed to promote health."

"I bet it was the Greens," said Claire, "it's always the Greens that are the killjoys. No meat, no cow milk, no travel, no pets, and they even tried to ban TDA."

"That's not fair," said Elaine. "You don't know it was them that stopped MedChips dealing with hangover symptoms. Also, the Greens were the ones that brought in the gender recognition and polygamy laws and they've always been supportive of the Brothel."

Elaine had been appointed as the judicial representative on the Brothel's Board of Management, and she felt duty-bound to defend its interests.

"True," said Claire, "the Greens aren't killjoys when it comes to sex. Just everything else."

"So, what did we find out?" asked Victoria to change the subject.

Elaine had been recording their findings on a sheet of paper. She preferred an old-fashioned pen and paper to an app on her phone.

"David, Roger and I went to five off-licences each, so fifteen off-licences total. We bought a bottle of the ten-year-old Glencarbost at all of them and also a bottle of a random different type of whisky. Claire and Victoria went round all the bars near the arcade. Victoria bought Glencarbost and Claire another type of whisky. They took a sample from each glass in a test tube."

"We didn't actually buy the drinks ourselves," said Claire. "Mostly guys bought them for us."

"And what's the result?"

"Justine smelled E511 in five out of the fifteen bottles of Glencarbost, but none of the other bottled whiskies."

"What about the glasses from the pubs?"

"I'm less confident about that data. Justine started to take sneaky licks of the samples. By the end of the night, she was running in circles and chasing her tail."

"Tell us anyway."

"We had forty test tubes. Justine says five of them were ten-year-old Glencarbost and one of those contained E511. Of the other 35, none of them had E511. Most of them smelled like blended whisky, not single malt."

"Which off-licences and bars did the samples with E511 come from?" asked Roger.

The others groaned.

"OK, we should probably have labelled them," said Claire, "but we've still learned three things. First, about thirty percent of the bottles of 10-year-old Glencarbost in central Edinburgh are watered down, second it doesn't look like any other brand is being tampered with, and third you can't trust boys you met in a bar to come back with the drink you asked for."

"Valuable lessons," said Victoria, "and also it wasn't a bad night out."

— ♦ —

Downstairs in the arcade office, James had spent all night playing TDA with his friends, Milton and Alexandra. They'd just finished robbing a bank on Hollywood Boulevard after multiple attempts and were now sitting in Alexandra's apartment in Los Espíritus, discussing what to do next.

Alexandra walked over to the window and looked out over the marina.

"I love this apartment," she said. "I always wanted to stay here, and it is so much nicer since James and Anthony modded it for me so the windows work and I have full control of the furniture and decorations."

"It's just a two-bedroom apartment with a small garage," said Milton. "There are much nicer places in the game. You could have a penthouse in the Casino or a superyacht."

"The location is perfect for me. I can see the sailboats out the window and my motorcycle club is just a couple of blocks away, near the beach."

"The thing I don't understand," said Milton, "is why you are even bothering with a motorcycle club. There are much easier ways of making money. In fact, I don't know why you even stay in this game at all now that TDA 6 is out."

Alexandra smiled.

"It's not about getting finished quickly," she said. "I'm in no rush. I want to play through legitimately and see everything there is. Once I've got everything in the game, I'll move on to something else."

"You'll get bored," said Milton.

"Maybe," she said, "and if that happens, I'll finish it up and move on. But right now I'm enjoying starting from scratch. It's OK to just have a two-bedroom apartment and a motorbike and make my money doing deliveries. You miss a lot if you skip things just because the money isn't as good. I like driving a motorbike into Los Espíritus from the desert with a great song on the radio and the sun coming up."

"Yeah, it's fun the first time," said Milton, "but not the hundredth. And while you are doing the first run, some guy like me will be sitting in their submarine firing missiles at your parked delivery vehicles."

"That was you!" she shouted. "You bastard. It took a week to get that delivery ready. I can't afford equipment and staff yet."

"Sorry," said Milton.

Alexandra pulled herself together.

"It's OK," she said. "Being griefed is part of doing MC deliveries, and I wouldn't want to miss anything."

Her voice hardened. "As long as it doesn't happen too often."

Milton noticed her change in tone.

"Of course not, Alexandra. I promise I won't grief you again, and if you need someone to help with your deliveries, just ask."

"Thanks," said Alexandra, "you're a pal. It's always better with more people when I get the vans. James, would you help too? I think

I am going to get post vans again."

"Why do you think it will be post vans?" asked James. "You don't see what vehicle you'll get until you start the mission."

Alexandra's brow furrowed.

"Sometimes I'm just fairly sure of something. I don't know why, and I'm not always right, but usually when I'm sure of something, then that's what happens."

"That's how thinking works," said Milton. "If a neural network gets enough training data, then after a while it will recognise patterns and get better at making predictions."

"So, Milton," said James, "you are an artificial life form based on an electronic neural network. Do you know when you are going to get post vans? Because my biological neurons certainly don't."

"No," said Milton, "but there are two reasons for that. First, I don't care if I get post vans, if it happens I just swap sessions and pay the fine, so my brain is not going to devote a lot of resources to that question. And second, I never play MC missions in the first place because the money is rubbish. Therefore, I have insufficient training data."

"But you've been playing TDA non stop for about ten years," said James. "Alexandra is just starting out. Even though you usually avoid MC sales, you will have more training data than Alexandra. So why can her neural net work it out and yours can't?"

"Humph," said Milton. "You really haven't figured it out yet, have you?"

"What?"

"The Alexandras cooperate. Alexandra can predict there will be post vans even though she's hardly done any MC sales herself because her neural network is intertwined with the neural networks of all the other Alexandras. Between them, they have done hundreds of thousands, probably millions of MC deliveries and they have more than enough data to evolve a neural network that can predict what vehicle they will get. Your brain needs to fit in your head and mine needs to fit in an accelerator card in a PC, but the Alexandras' brains are spread out across an entire data centre. Our brains need to prioritise how a limited number of neurons are used. When Alexandra gets close to running out of neurons, the Guild buys more computers."

Alexandra smiled.

"I'm not a scientist. I don't know about neural networks and how thinking works. Sometimes I know things and I couldn't tell you how I know them. Enough talk. Let's sell my forged documents."

"You're a four dimensional hyper intelligence and you are selling forged documents with post vans!" said Milton incredulously.

"I told you before, it's not about money. I want to try everything in the game."

"OK then," said James. "I'll help with your sale. But first I need to take a bathroom break and get some coffee; we've been playing all night."

"Good idea," said Milton. "There's no way we can do this when you are half asleep."

"Be nice, Milton," said Alexandra. "You need to make allowances for biological people. And don't worry James, if you help me I'll help you with something in your game too. It's only fair."

— ♦ —

Bleary-eyed, Justine slunk downstairs and soon found the staff toilets. As promised, there was a shower cubicle. The seat on the toilet had been left up, which she assumed was due to its last user being James, the arcade owner. James slept on a camp bed in the office: there was no point spending money renting a flat when he spent all his free time playing TDA and the best computers for playing TDA were in the arcade. Justine was too hungover and had too much alcohol left in her system to worry much about anything except the necessities. Her cat side seemed to be competing with her human side for control this morning. The playful Labrador was nowhere to be seen. The cat hated showers but was willing to make an exception when its fur was this disgusting. So she pulled off her clothes, dropped them on the floor of the bathroom, and turned on the water. She'd have preferred the shower a little bit stronger and a little bit warmer, but all new showers were like this thanks to EU rules on water consumption and energy use. Justine snorted: like Scotland had any shortage of rain and wind power. But there was one standard for the whole of Europe: the southern countries had problems with water shortages and Germany and Poland had problems with energy supply now that they couldn't use gas, coal or nuclear. There were shower gel and shampoo bottles in the shower, probably James's, but Justine didn't care as long as they got the remnants of last night out of her fur. She didn't mind mud or natural smells from the forest, but the smell of an ancient sofa in a coffee bar wasn't pleasant.

She finished up and stepped out of the shower. There was no towel. In her hungover state, she'd not thought of that. But her cat side wasn't putting up with wet fur any longer. She twisted her torso from side to side, shaking the water off. A cascade of water droplets landed on the floor of the bathroom.

In the arcade office, James took off his headphones and Virtual Reality glasses and looked at the clock on his computer. It was only 6 a.m., Claire wouldn't turn up to open the arcade for business for another three hours. He should get a shower and a pee as well as a coffee and his morning Fuel before getting back to the game.

James sniffed his T-shirt and tried to remember when he'd last changed clothes. He wasn't sure, but it definitely wasn't yesterday. When it came to housework, James was a great believer in minimisation of effort, so he stripped off and chucked his clothes in the laundry basket before going for his shower. Sleepily, he shuffled out of the office and across to the staff toilet.

"Arrgggggh!" There was a huge cat in the arcade bathroom.

Justine was pre-occupied with shaking the water from her fur. It took a full second for her to notice a man was coming into the toilet. Instinctively, she pounced on the incomer and knocked him to the floor.

Justine had timed her pounce perfectly. James was flat on his back. She was directly above him with her forepaws on his shoulders. Fortunately, she had not been sufficiently alarmed to extend her claws.

After a split second, the cat side of Justine recognised what had happened, and it decided the situation was amusing and should be prolonged. The first thing was to get a proper smell of the male she was pinning to the floor. Cats have a secondary olfactory organ on the roof of their mouth. It is wired into their brain differently from their nose, and its primary function is to sniff other cats and cat urine to determine their mating status. Unfortunately for James, in order to use this organ, cats open their mouth wide and pull back their lips, exposing their teeth. Justine had some quite impressive teeth.

James lay on his back on the tiled floor. He didn't seem to have hurt himself seriously when he was knocked over, but the huge cat was now directly above him and baring its teeth. Not good. But it wasn't biting, and a few seconds later, it closed its mouth. James started to pay more attention. The cat's face had much less fur on it than the rest of its body. One day's growth since Justine hadn't had time to remove it. The face was human and female and now the mouth was closed and the teeth were out of the way, attractive. Then James noticed the cat had breasts and its legs were pressed against his.

Justine's cat side decided to make friends and began to push against James' shoulders with its paws, first one, then the other. Maybe this human could be persuaded to brush her fur. It was wet and tangled and could really use brushed out. She already had three human friends who were willing to groom her upstairs, but another one was always useful.

James realised the human cat was friendly and as soon as he stopped being scared, his body responded to being pinned to the floor by a naked female. Oh shit! But it was literally out of his hands. There was nothing he could do, except stay still and hope the cat wouldn't bite or scratch.

Fortunately for James, Justine's cat side was in control and cats are not well known for sexual propriety. She felt something touch her and looked down.

"Miaow!" said Justine.

James's eyes opened wide in fear.

"Sorry!" he said, "but you're lying on top of me. I can't control it."

The cat thought the situation was funny. Also, when it caught something, it liked to play.

"Victoria told me you were a virgin," it said.

James nodded. "Yes," but then to mitigate the charge he added, "but my female identity isn't, and I have lots of friends online."

"Well," said the cat, "this is an interesting situation. Seeing as you are a virgin. Look at my face, don't look down. Or I'll scratch."

James was very careful not to look down.

"I can feel your erection. It's touching me in exactly the right spot," said the cat. "But I can't tell if the tip has actually passed my labia. If it has, then you aren't a virgin anymore." Then Justine remembered the Guild science classes she'd taken. "What we have here is a quantum defloration situation: Schrödinger's pussy. If you look down and observe what's happening, you're sure to get harder, and the system will resolve into the deflowered state."

"So, are you Schrödinger's cat?" asked James.

"Technically, I am a human, cat, Labrador chimaera," said Justine. She decided she'd teased James long enough and pushed herself up on her forepaws and rolled carefully off. "But I prefer the term were-Labracat. I'm Justine. I'm friends with Victoria and Claire, and we've met before when I was in the police."

"Sorry, I remember now. I didn't recognise you before because I was distracted by the fur and the tail. And the teeth."

"It's OK, but I hope we can be friends and that you'll keep my secret about the fur and the tail."

"That seems fair, as long as you promise not to act like a cop when you are with me."

"Deal! In any case, I was fired. I'm not a cop anymore. I'm a sheriff's officer."

The Debutante Draft

As usual, Justine woke at first light. She was in her basket in the kitchen of her husband's town house in Moray Place. Usually, she'd have been quiet, maybe gone out for a quick prowl along the gorge of Leith Water behind their house, perhaps catch a rabbit. But today was different. They were going to the Royal Highland Show, and Justine was excited. She gave her fur a quick lick, drank some water, and went upstairs to her husband's bedroom. She jumped straight onto the bed.

"What the fuck, Justine? It's 6a.m.!"

"Come on, come on, get up. It'll take you ages to get ready, and I need to be there early!"

Her husbands were almost as excited about the show as she was, so there wasn't too much complaining.

"Alright, alright, we're coming. Put on the coffee. We'll be down in a minute."

Justine made coffee and some porridge for herself while her husbands and son drank their morning Fuel. She would have preferred some rabbit or deer, and there was some left in the fridge from her last hunt, but there was no time to cook it. Raw meat didn't bother her at all, but her family, point blank, refused to let her eat like that at the table.

As she had predicted, it took some considerable time to get ready. By rights, as the only family member with fur, she should have been the last to finish. After all, she had to carefully shave the fur from her face before going out and tape her tail down. On the other hand, she wasn't dressing up like a New Georgian. She had her hiking boots, combat trousers, a long-sleeved technical T-shirt, and a soft shell with plenty of pockets. In contrast, Elaine was wearing a frock straight out of a costume drama. Henry had a suit with a top hat and her son Robert was dressed like a miniaturised version of his father. Usually Elaine would have complained about Justine's attire when representing the family on an occasion such as this, but there were special circumstances today. This was the Royal Highland Show, the premier annual meeting of the landed gentry, and the outdoor clothing signified that Justine was not there as a gawking townie. She was taking part in the business of the show.

It was already eight o'clock by the time they were ready to leave, and Justine was starting to fret.

"Woof!"

"Alright, alright, you can summon a car," said Elaine. "We'll be ready before it gets here."

— ♦ —

The Royal Highland Show was the last bastion of the landed aristocracy and hadn't quite caught up with 21st century technology. After confirming her identity with an iris scan in the registration tent, Justine was presented with an official badge to wear. A real, printed paper badge with a blue tab in one corner. The badge said 'Ms Justine Claverhouse' and underneath 'Claverhouse and Company' and the blue tab indicated she was registered to bid at auctions. Not only that, but Alexandra had managed to get Claverhouse and Company a contract as a security consultant to the show, so she was also issued with a hi-viz vest with 'Show Security' on the back. It was all very exciting, especially when you were having a Labrador day.

Justine stowed the vest in her backpack and put on her badge. The first order of business was to find the auction yard. The show was far smaller now than in its heyday before farming animals was banned. The organisers had done their best and created almost mud-free gravel paths between the sheds and tents, and provided pristine white tarpaulin roofs over the routes the King would need to use. The agricultural equipment and livestock auction wasn't in the posh part of the show, though. It was out of sight, away from the VIPs, and there were no freshly laid gravel paths. It was concrete yards and muddy paddocks. But Justine didn't care because she could see the horses.

Her phone rang; it was her assistant, Alexandra.

"I want to see too!"

Justine had forgotten all about Alexandra.

"Sorry, I got carried away! I can see the horses."

"Let me see too," sulked Alexandra. "I may be dead and a disembodied consciousness, but I still like horses."

Justine put her Bluetooth earpiece in and clipped her small body-cam to her jacket.

"Can you see now?"

"Yes, go on then, go to the paddock."

Justine ran over to the paddock. It would have been more professional to walk, but her Labrador side was having none of that. There were six horses in the paddock and one of them was bright silver. It looked exactly like Justine's friend Andy - except that Andy was a unicorn and this horse didn't have a horn, and Andy was a boy and this one was a girl. Justine and Andy had played together on her aunt's farm when she was a teenager. As soon as Justine approached the gate, the silver horse walked over and let her pat it.

"You've got to buy that one," said Alexandra in her ear "It's beautiful."

Justine had made her mind up about that the second she saw it.

"Alexandra, you're supposed to be the smart one. You're supposed to be making sure I don't spend too much. It feels like a Labrador day today, and Labradors aren't very good with money."

"Don't worry, it'll be fine. You can afford a horse."

"Are you sure?"

"Do you know how much we made on the British Museum repossession job?"

"No, you never told me."

"Well, to be honest, I don't know either, so many of the objects are nearly impossible to value. But our fee is 2% and my guess is when it is all worked out there'll be between ten and twenty billion euros worth of recovered property. So I'm fairly sure you can afford a horse."

"OK then!"

"In any case, it is an investment. If we can get you into the forest on horseback and you can bring back four or five fugitives on each trip instead of just one, we can make more profit on bounty-hunting jobs. So go and look at the lorries, too."

Justine patted the silver horse and went to look for the yard with the agricultural machinery. In among the electric tractors and combine harvesters were two extremely old lorries. The smaller lorry was a transporter for police horses. The second one was a large articulated lorry with a detachable cab. The trailer was a mobile police station complete with a small office, crew rest area, and a cell. The lorries were so old they ran on diesel; the bodywork was rusted, and the cab for the mobile police station had slumped down in one corner like there was a problem with the suspension. The trailer wasn't in much better condition. But all the Labrador side of Justine was interested in was the flashing blue light strips and POLICE markings. They were so cool.

Someone from the auction company came over. He was wearing a green fleece with the company's name embroidered on the left side and wellingtons.

"Are you interested in the old police mounted section vehicles? They're up for sale, along with the last of their horses and tack. Budget cuts."

Justine nodded.

"Well, they're being sold as-is. They're historic vehicles so you can run them off diesel legally, if you can find any diesel, that is. It's a few years since the cops used them and they don't have a current MOT, so you'll need to fix them up before taking them on the road."

"Can you give me a test drive?"

"They're not self driving. If you've got a licence to drive a lorry this size yourself and you've got some diesel to put in them, you're welcome to try, as long as you stay in the showground. They're not road legal."

Justine shook her head.

"How much are they?"

"It's an auction, depends on what people bid," said the man. "How much do you think thirty-year-old lorries nobody can drive, it's near impossible to get fuel for and that will cost a fortune to fix up before they are legal on the roads are worth?"

"Say 10,000," said Alexandra in her earpiece.

"I'll give you 10,000 euro, 15,000 if you throw in the horses."

"Doesn't work like that. Like I said, it's an auction. Highest bidder."

"Tell him you can't attend the auction and walk away," said Alexandra.

"That's a shame," said Justine. "I'd have liked to bid, but my company is providing security for the show and I'm about to go on duty." She took the 'Show Security' vest out of her backpack to illustrate her point.

"Hold on, 15,000 cash? And you'll shift them today?"

"15,000 cash for both trucks and the horses, and I'll get back to you about where to deliver them."

"It'll be another thousand for delivery. They'll need towed."

"Deal. My assistant will call you to make the arrangements for the funds transfer and handle the paperwork."

As Justine left the auction company's yard, despite the enthusiasm of her Labrador side, she couldn't help wondering if she had just done something very stupid. She lived in a basket in her husband's kitchen - where was she going to keep six horses and two lorries?

— ♦ —

Naturally, Justine returned immediately to the horses and climbed the gate to get a closer look at her purchases.

"Can you ride the silver horse?" asked Alexandra.

"I don't think they'll let me ride without a saddle."

"I've been talking to the other Alexandras," said Alexandra. "We're all very excited."

Justine hadn't realised that the Alexandras talked amongst themselves about her business. She wasn't sure she approved.

"We don't tell each other secrets," said Alexandra, "but we all started out as copies of the same person's consciousness. We're like twin sisters."

"I suppose so," said Justine. "I hadn't thought about it."

"Anyway," said Alexandra, "Your aunt's Alexandra says you can keep the horses on the farm and your uncle's Alexandra says if you bring the lorries to the Guild's old office near Ratho his robotics firm will fix them up for you."

"Did your sisters ask my aunt and uncle? I already owe my aunt a favour for helping with the cheese making and I owe my uncle a huge favour for arranging the equipment to move the British Museum."

"They haven't asked yet, but it will be alright. Your aunt and uncle let their Alexandras handle most things for them."

"I feel I am imposing, asking too many favours," said Justine.

"It doesn't cost your uncle anything to let you use his empty shed. And he really loves customising and improving things. He'll have a lot of fun upgrading your trucks. And your aunt likes horses. She will be happy to have a few on her farm."

"But I feel I should do something for them in return."

"Buying horses and lorries will help Madame Noyce catch the runaways in the forest faster. You will enjoy the horses and make a profit. Your aunt will like having horses on her farm. Your uncle will enjoy tinkering with and improving the vehicles. I am sure that when you buy the horses, the sum of happiness of Guild members will increase."

Justine's human side couldn't help thinking that there was something not quite right about the Alexandras collaborating to maximise the happiness of Guild members. But her human side was quickly outvoted: the Labrador wanted a horse and the cat couldn't care less about moral philosophy.

"Maybe you're right," said Justine. "But I know my uncle and he sometimes gets carried away with his improvements, so please ask him not to install Guild technology in the lorries. They'll be transporting prisoners, and prisoners don't keep their mouths shut."

— ♦ —

Justine was kept busy with her show security job all morning; Elaine was taking part in the homemade cheese competition and the rest of the family was spectating. After lunch, at two p.m. the final judging was about to start. It was one of the most prestigious events in the show and held in a large marquee conveniently positioned near the refreshment tent. The judges had whittled the field down over the morning, and only the top ten contestants remained. Each contestant stood behind a display table decked with crisp white linen. The contestants had been required to bring exactly one kilogram of their product, but after the preliminary judging rounds, only about half remained. Beside the cheese on the table, the organisers had provided a plate of wafer biscuits and a cheese knife and three small side plates, one for each of the three judges.

Elaine, Madame l'Hôpital and Mrs Bunnet had arrived early and taken tables next to each other at the quieter end of the marquee, farthest away from the entrance. The judges arrived ten minutes late and carrying flutes of champagne and small bowls of strawberries and cream. They stood near the entrance of the tent, chatting to each other and ignoring the contestants until their strawberries were finished. The table next to Mrs Bunnet was empty, but as the judges finished their drinks, a young woman broke away from their party and took her place behind it, she was followed by a butler in a formal grey suit carrying a wicker hamper. The butler set out the cheese sample on the table and replaced the provided plates, crackers, and utensils with his own superior versions.

Elaine scowled, but was too polite to say anything. The judges split up and made their way through the tables one by one, tasting and taking notes. The first judge was tall, jovial, and wearing chef's whites. As he approached, Elaine could see the embroidered script on his uniform bearing the name of the most famous French restaurant in Edinburgh. The man cleansed his palate with champagne, spread a cracker with her cheese, sniffed, and then nibbled. When he was finished, he said 'Thank you', photographed the cheese, wrote a note on his iPad and moved to the next table. His face was completely emotionless throughout. Elaine had not the slightest inkling of his thoughts on her produce. In her career as a judge, Elaine had seen many lawyers and defendants try to maintain a poker face during a trial and she could usually see through it, but not this time.

The second judge was Jack McCallister, leader of the Pàrtaidh Tòraidheach na h-Alba and recent entrant to the landowning classes following his purchase of Cockpen Estate. Mr McCallister was easier to read than the Chef. He chatted, swigged champagne and had three crackers deeply spread with her precious cheese. Unlike the Chef, Mr McCallister saw no need for tasting notes or photographs. He simply made a token wave with one hand, held out his glass to a passing waiter for a refill, and moved to the next table.

The third judge, Mr Ross Murray, was the scion of one of the wealthiest landowning families in Scotland. He had watched the chef and attempted to duplicate his procedure, photographing the cheese, before cleansing his palette, taking a sample on a cracker, sniffing and finally nibbling. But he hadn't got the memo on maintaining a poker face.

"Oh, that's absolutely delicious," he said. "That's even better than the Roquefort they had at the Ritz the last time I was in London. You better watch you don't get arrested: this is too good not to be cow's milk!"

Elaine blushed.

"It's all completely legal, I assure you, the cheese was made from my own milk collected at the City Farm. I have all the necessary records if you would like to see them."

"That won't be necessary," said the young man. "We're all property owners and gentlefolk. We can trust each other!"

Elaine was disappointed: her heart had risen when she thought she'd be required to display her meticulously collated paperwork.

As the last judge moved on, Elaine exchanged glances with Mrs Bunnet and Madame l'Hôpital. None of them were any the wiser as to who might have won.

At the far end of the tent, the butler who had set out the table next to Madame l'Hôpital was being given orders by a severe-looking woman in her sixties. He came over with his wicker basket, tidied away the superior cutlery and biscuits, and collected the remains of the cheese. He seemed in a hurry to remove everything as quickly as possible. As the butler finished up, his mistress moved across and joined the small group of judges. They'd been chatting together before the judging commenced and she seemed to see nothing inappropriate about joining them again before the verdicts were delivered. The judges stood around talking among themselves, apparently waiting for something. Finally, the reason for the delay became clear. Justine arrived in her 'Show Security' vest accompanying one of the stewards, who was carrying a briefcase. The rosettes and medals had arrived!

The stewards built a mini podium from three wooden boxes, the show photographer got ready to take pictures, and Jack McCallister moved to the front of the room.

"First of all, I'd like to say we have had an exceptionally high standard of produce this year and the judging task has been particularly difficult. However, after some debate, we have reached a decision."

He paused.

"In third place, with the Blue Lanark Roquefort, Justice Elaine Cockburn."

Her heart swelling with pride, Elaine stepped forward and took her place on the smallest of the wooden boxes. Mr McCallister pinned the Bronze medal to her chest and handed her a white rosette.

"In second place, with the Farmhouse Cheddar, Countess Bunnet!"

There was muted applause and Mrs Bunnet came forward to collect her medal.

"And in first place, with the most delectable Stilton it has ever been my pleasure to taste, Miss Anne Bampot."

The severe-looking lady at the back clapped loudly and the surrounding party followed suit as the winner came forward to claim her prize.

With the safe delivery of the medals, Justine's job was done, but her nose was twitching. She walked the length of the tent, approaching each table in turn, and paused at the empty table next to Madame l'Hôpital.

"I smell Stilton," she said to Madame l'Hôpital, "who was using this table?"

"That's her," said Madame l'Hôpital, "the one on top of the podium. Her mother is friends with the judges."

"What happened to her cheese?" asked Justine, "this doesn't smell like human milk."

"Cleared away," said Madame l'Hôpital with disgust, "a servant in a grey suit, he packed it up into a hamper the second the judging was finished."

Justine left the tent at a run, shouting instructions into her radio.

After the medal ceremony, Elaine was clearing away and commiserating with Madame l'Hôpital for not winning anything when the Chef came over.

"Mesdames," he said, "I must congratulate you on a most exquisite Roquefort and a Brie which would not be out of place in my mother's kitchen."

The ladies thanked him for his kind words.

"In my opinion," he went on, "the Roquefort was the fromage supérieur this afternoon and the Brie à la deuxième place. Unfortunately, I was overruled by the other judges. I informed them the Stilton was made with cow's milk, but they refused to listen. I have two Michelin stars and a diploma from the Institute de Fromage de France, but I am overruled by a politician and a landowner."

"Sacrebleu!" said Madame l'Hôpital, "Menteurs, tricheurs!"

"Here is my card," said the Chef and bowed to Elaine. "If you ever decide to have the Roquefort made commercially, I would be very interested in securing a supply for my restaurant."

Meanwhile, in the car park, the butler had been stopped by show security and an altercation was developing as Justine arrived.

"I need to see inside that hamper," she demanded.

"Absolutely not," replied the butler. "You are not a police officer, you have no right to search my property."

"That's easily fixed," said Justine and got on her radio.

Soon a Europol biosecurity officer and a Police Scotland sergeant arrived on the scene. They took Justine aside.

"Do you know who that is, Justine?" asked the sergeant.

"No idea. But I have reason to believe that he has Stilton cheese made with cow's milk in that hamper."

The Europol officer sighed.

"No shit, Sherlock!" he said. "That's Lady Bampot's butler. Her yacht is docked at Leith and it will be packed full of animal foodstuffs from Hunsford, her estate in England. But we can't touch her."

"If you search that hamper, you'll find enough Stilton to put him away."

"Yeah, but we aren't going to search it," said the sergeant, "do you know who Lady Bampot is?"

"Isn't she the wife of Baron Jesse 'Bagger' Bampot the English excavator magnate?" said Justine.

"You really don't have a clue, do you? Don't you watch 'Scotland's Next Royal'?"

"I'm not that interested in royals," said Justine.

"The very first series, right after independence, she won. In those days, it was the King himself who married the winner. Of course, the series kept running and he married plenty of other people after that. After a few years, she took Bagger Bampot as her second husband and moved away to England. In the early days of the show, they'd not thought of post-dated divorces. So, even though they've not lived together for twenty years, she's still married to the King. Police Scotland aren't about to arrest the Queen's butler for a few hundred grammes of dodgy cheese!"

"As the wife of a head of state, Lady Bampot has diplomatic immunity," added the Europol officer, "Europol can't touch her."

— ♦ —

As usual, the highlight of the last day of the Royal Highland Show was the debutantes' draft. The focus had moved from the showground beside the airport to the elegant Assembly Rooms in George Street. The guests spread out in small groups across a hundred banquet tables with linen tablecloths, uniformed waiters served champagne. And on a raised dais at the far end of the hall, the King sat with the President of the Royal Highland Society, Baron Trevor Minto. To the King's right, a seat of honour had been provided for the event's sponsor, the reclusive heiress Victoria Campbell, but it was empty. To their left, a floor-to-ceiling video screen was showing highlights of the previous year's draft. The sound was switched off but the host of TV's Reporting Scotland was standing ready to act as compere for the evening as soon as everyone was seated.

Finally, the doors were closed, and the lights went down. Everyone stood for the National Anthem, which was led by a soprano from Scottish Opera.

"... and sent him homewards, to think again!" she finished.

The audience gave a round of applause and resumed their seats.

"My Lords, Ladies and Gentlemen - The King!"

King Charles took to his feet and made his way to a gilded lectern.

"Welcome everyone to the 15th annual Debutantes' Draft. I want to thank you particularly for bringing your young people, future landowners and aristocrats to our celebration. It was a pleasure to be introduced to them all at court over the last few days, and I'm sure they will make excellent matches. And now, without further ado, let the 2047 Debutante's Draft begin!"

'Also Sprach Zarathustra' belted out of the sound system, lasers flashed and the President of the Royal Highland Society took to his feet.

"How does this draft work?" Madame l'Hôpital asked Elaine. "In France we have an auction. Do the debutantes have to marry these men?"

"Oh, of course not," said Elaine. "After the draft, the debutantes are merely betrothed for one year. If they can't come to personal terms with their fiancé during that time and no marriage is concluded, they can enter next year's draft as free agents."

"So they can't marry anyone else for a year?"

"Not unless their fiancé trades them: there's a lot of trading goes on after the couples get to know each other. And of course, some selections are made purely as an investment with the intention of trading for something else."

They stopped talking as the Royal Highland Show President came to the microphone.

"As usual, the most wealthy guests will pick first. I am informed that we have an unexpected guest tonight, Mr Arseny Parslikov, a businessman and bachelor from Russia who, according to Forbes Magazine, has a business empire worth five trillion euros. As a gesture of Scottish hospitality, and in honour of his great wealth, the committee has decided to offer Mr Parslikov the first pick."

There was a round of applause and all eyes turned to Lady Bampot's table, where Mr Parslikov was seated beside her ladyship's daughter. His neighbours attempted to persuade him to stand up and were eventually successful, although judging by his countenance, Mr Parslikov was not best pleased.

"I am not acquainted with any of these ladies." he said. "It would be insupportable to choose a future partner at a provincial assembly such as this. Therefore, I decline your offer."

Stunned silence descended on the room. The debutantes and their relations were mortified. Even the King's face, normally a model of diplomatic tact, expressed shock and displeasure.

After a few seconds, the President of the Highland Society composed himself. He decided the best thing was to act as though the incident had never occurred and continue without further comment.

"In that case, the first pick of the evening goes to the generous sponsor of tonight's event, Ms Victoria Campbell, owner of Argyll Lettings, with a personal net worth estimated at three trillion euros."

There was a round of polite applause led by the King tapping his index and middle fingers delicately against the palm of his left hand.

The President read from a card he'd been handed.

"With the first pick, Ms Campbell selects Miss Elizabeth Bunnet. Tight End Receiver."

The music and lights started up again as Miss Bunnet walked to the front of the room and was presented with a dark blue Scotland shirt with the number one on the back to pull over her ballgown.

Justine turned to Elaine.

"Why would Victoria pick her? I never thought she was interested in getting married."

"She's probably going to trade her," said Elaine wisely, "the rumour is that the Bunnet sisters have got licences to procreate. All the aristocratic families will be trying to get one in the draft. It's been years since any of the top four families have managed to produce an heir."

"I read about the Bunnets in the Milngavie and Morningside Messenger," said Justine's second husband, Henry, "the family was visiting a Russian friend's estate in Tuscany when that terrible earthquake happened."

"Belmont," said Elaine, "the entire village was destroyed."

"That's it, and to restore the population, the Italian government gave every surviving female in Belmont district an exemption from compulsory birth control. As long as they keep their Italian Med-Chips, they will be fertile until they have their first child."

They stopped talking as the President was handed the second card.

"The second pick of the evening goes to Mr Trevor Minto, heir to the Minto estates with a personal net worth estimated at one trillion euro."

Mr Minto got somewhat more enthusiastic applause than Victoria, led by a contingent from the Pàrtaidh Tòraidheach na h-Alba.

"With the second pick," the President paused for silence.

"With the second pick, Mr Minto selects Miss Jane Bunnet."

"Told you the Bunnet sisters would be drafted first," whispered the Sheriff.

The President was moving along faster now. There were a hundred debutantes and free agents to get through and after the draft for first wives, there would also be a draft for second and third wives.

"The third pick goes to Mr Ross Murray, heir to Highland estates, covering 100,000 hectares with an estimated value of 500 million euro."

He picked up the card.

"With the third pick, Mr Murray selects… Miss Mary Bunnet."

"The fourth pick goes to Baron Jesse Bampot, founder of Bampot excavators and Chairman of Bampot Baggers AG with an estimated personal net worth of 300 million euro. It will be made by his wife, Baroness Bampot."

"With the fourth pick, Baroness Bampot selects Miss Catherine Bunnet."

The fifth pick was also a Bunnet sister. Lydia Bunnet was chosen by Mr Richard Seuchar.

The President waited for the applause to die down.

"And now, Ladies and Gentlemen, The King!"

A footman banged the floor three times with a ceremonial mace while a second footman placed the crown on the King's head. The King stood, and a robe of ermine was placed over his shoulders. He was handed a parchment and began to read the Latin text. Fortunately, the compere had been provided with a translation and informed the audience in hushed tones.

"As is the tradition, His Majesty is now asserting his right under the ancient law of Jus Primae Noctis. The fortunate brides in the first five places of the draft will spend their wedding night with the King!"

"He used to manage the first ten," whispered Elaine to Justine, "but he's getting older now."

— ♦ —

Within a short walk of Jambourn lived a family with whom the Bunnets were particularly intimate. Sir William Cunningham Lycass had made his fortune before independence in the executive portable lavatory business providing conveniences for prestigious outdoor events such as golf tournaments and royal garden parties. This latter engagement had led to Sir William's company - Larkhall Lavvies Ltd. - being awarded a Royal Warrant which it had emblazoned on the doors of the pickup truck which transported the pump and tank used to empty their porta-potties. In the interests of decorum, for royal engagements the shit-tank was covered in a crocheted pink antimacassar with a union jack motif. After being knighted for his services to the lavatorial industry, Sir William - WC to his friends - grew tired of the world of business and sold out to the German conglomerate Schrobenhausen Scheisshausen GmbH. He now lived the life of a gentleman of leisure, seeking only to make friends with influential people and use his connections to further his sizeable investment portfolio.

Sir William's wife, Colonel Ruth Lycass, was a former colleague of Mrs Bunnet in the English House of Lords and a close friend. Like many Tory politicians prior to independence, she'd been awarded an honorary military rank for spending two weeks answering the phones for the Territorial Army and being friends with the Secretary of State for Defence. The Lycasses had one child, Michael Charlotte Lycass, known to her friends as Charlie. MC Lycass was the DJ at the Gosvenor Club in the New Town, where she did a thriving trade supplying cocaine to the upper classes. Charlie was Elizabeth Bunnet's best friend and confidante.

That the Bunnets and the Lycasses should meet to discuss the events of the Debutante's Draft was absolutely necessary. Therefore, the next day, the Bunnet ladies walked to Lycass Lodge, a large villa on a secluded street in Duddingston near the entrance to Holyrood Park.

"You began the evening well, Eliza," said Mrs Lycass. "You were the very first pick. And Victoria Campbell too, the richest woman in Scotland."

"Yes, but Mr Arseny Parslikov refused to pick anyone at all. By rights, Ms Campbell should have had the second pick!" said Elizabeth.

"I must say," said Mrs Bunnet, although clearly she was under no obligation to say anything, "the behaviour of Mr Parslikov was intolerable, and that of the entire party around Baroness Bampot was rude in the extreme."

"Certainly," said Mrs Lycass, "if Mr Parslikov did not wish to participate in the draft he should not have attended, or informed the organisers privately in advance. To refuse to make a pick in such a proud and churlish manner is not the behaviour of a gentleman."

"And Lady Bampot, choosing to present her daughter at the English rather than the Scottish court, is no better."

"I have heard that Miss Anne Bampot has dual nationality since her mother is Scottish and her father is English and she was born in England. As an English citizen, she has no MedChip and can have children. If she stays in Scotland for more than a year, she would become a permanent resident and require a MedChip."

"The gossip in the Gosvenor Club is that Lady Bampot intends her daughter to marry Mr Parslikov. Apparently she had an understanding with Mr Parslikov's late father that the alliance between the families would be cemented by marriage," said Miss Lycass.

"That could explain why neither took part in the draft," said Mrs Bunnet, "but the manner of Mr Parslikov's refusal was arrogant."

"You may rest assured that if Mr Parslikov is too proud to select me at the first opportunity, he will not be given a second chance," said Elizabeth. "As for Ms Campbell. I was notified by the Debutante Draft website this morning that she has traded me to a gentleman called James Fergusson."

"I got traded too, mum," put in Kitty, "Baroness Bampot traded me to the old Tory we went to see the other day, McCallister."

"Yes, dear, Lady Bampot is McCallister's patron, of course she was using her pick on his behalf."

"There is a rumour that Ms Campbell has a secret partner and they have a child," said Mrs Lycass bringing the conversation back to Elizabeth. "I'm not surprised she is using her pick for trading purposes. Do you know anything about this Mr Fergusson?"

"Nothing at all. All I have from the Draft is the name and a business address in the Old Town."

"No doubt he will get in touch. And if he has the means to purchase the first pick from Ms Campbell, he must be a man of substance."

At this point, the discussion of Elizabeth's pick was concluded and good manners called for Mrs Bunnet to enquire about the gentleman who had chosen Miss Lycass. Unfortunately, this was impossible because Miss Lycass had not been eligible to take part in the draft. Under the Gender Identity Act, she was perfectly entitled to take part in the draft as a female despite being biologically male. However, she was also fifty-four years old, and she had already been presented many years previously. There was, as yet, no legal protection for age identification and the Draft had chosen to disregard the fact that she identified as twenty-four and refused her entry.

Kitty resolved the situation by changing to a less contentious subject.

"How about the Hearts?" she enquired.

— ♦ —

The fortunes of Heart of Midlothian Football Club proved to be of greater interest to the Bunnets than the Lycasses, and the visit concluded more quickly than usual. Elizabeth could see Charlotte was unhappy, and it was kinder not to overstay their welcome.

Their route home took them past the Sheep Heid pub and back towards Duddingston Road. The Sheep Heid was the oldest pub in Scotland and would have been remarkably convenient for the Lycasses and Bunnets but unfortunately, both Mrs Lycass and Mrs Bunnet were barred for life due to an embarrassing incident involving a former Conservative colleague.

When they reached Niddrie Mains Road, the party split up. Elizabeth and Kittie announced their intention of taking the bus into town. Lizzie had decided to seek out the Mr Fergusson who had acquired her pick and Mrs Bunnet had instructed Kittie she was to call on Mr McAllister.

Mrs Bunnet, Jane and Lydia continued home, but Mary turned left towards Niddrie Library, where she was a volunteer. This being 2047, the library did not have paper books, but it did have several computer labs which offered access to commercial databases and course material from major universities. It also had a maker space with 3D printers, numerically controlled lathes, and printed circuit assembly robots. This was Mary's home from home. As a volunteer librarian, she had unrestricted access to the equipment: a perk of being the person who was supposed to enforce lab rules was not having to obey them yourself.

Mary was a studious young person. Her mother considered her slow and uncreative, but actually she was careful and rigorous. She was interested in functionality, not decoration. When she designed something she intended it would work reliably, not merely look good. She had wanted to study engineering at Edinburgh University and she had the grades to get in, but her mother considered studying for academic qualifications a waste of time when one could simply lie about already having them. There was more money in marrying a rich landowner. At first Mary had been heartbroken, but then she had discovered the library. Rather than a formal curriculum, she could study whatever interested her. She had access to course materials from the best universities in the US and EU and she could use the 3D printers to build her designs. Along with the library, Mary had discovered the South East Edinburgh Recycling Centre, which was only a short walk through the woods from the Bunnet family's house. The father of one of her school friends worked there, and he and his colleagues were susceptible to bribery with ice cream. This was not just any recycling centre. South East Edinburgh contained the University Science Campus at King's Buildings and the research quarter around the National Hospital. For someone like Mary, preferential access to the equipment and materials discarded by the research labs was like being let loose in a toy shop.

Mary's principal contribution to the family business was the maintenance of their vintage ice-cream van. Although she had more advanced projects, she took this task seriously. She had overhauled the engine completely, replacing many of the parts with 3D printed versions using more modern materials, and she'd developed a process to convert cooking oil into fuel. The downside of this was the exhaust from the van smelled like a chip shop. The upside was that cooking oil was readily available and was not subject to the extreme level of taxation placed on fuel for internal combustion engines. This was also why converting cooking oil to fuel was illegal, as, indeed, was her decision to add tetraethyllead to improve performance. Mary's self-curated engineering curriculum focussed exclusively on the study of existing machinery, mathematics, chemistry and physics and had no time for the tax, safety and environmental regulations which attempted to limit her design freedom.

— ♦ —

Elizabeth stepped out of the bus on South Bridge. Her new fiancé, Mr James Fergusson, was the proprietor of the Old School Arcade and she knew exactly where that was - right across from the stop, she got off the bus on the way to the milking parlour. Miss Bunnet had not been sure what the appropriate attire for the first meeting with a fiancé was and so she had consulted Lady Deborah Rettie's Guide for Wives and Gentlewomen and learned that while a full ballgown would be overly formal, casual clothing was out of the question. Accordingly, she'd borrowed one of her mother's dresses from the days of the family's prosperity. It was Armani, dark blue, tight, but not excessively so, and cut a little above the knee. Enough to pique the interest of a suitor should they prove desirable, but not enough to lead one on who was not.

First impressions of her beau's residence were not favourable. She'd hoped for a mansion set in substantial grounds, or perhaps a yacht: she might have accepted a detached house in the Grange or Barnton. She'd not expected an amusement arcade and cafe on South

Bridge. However, she had entered the Draft, and was subject to its rules. Like it or not, she was betrothed until either they married, her new fiancé traded her to another, or a year passed. Waiting a year was out of the question. She required a husband by the end of the summer.

"Excuse me," she said to the woman behind the counter. "I am looking for Mr Fergusson."

Claire was taken aback.

"You're looking for James?"

Elizabeth had forgotten her new fiancé's first name.

"Mr Fergusson, the owner. Can you tell him Elizabeth Bunnet is here?"

Claire figured it probably wouldn't be a good thing to show this fashionably dressed and perfumed lady into an office which smelled like somebody had lived there twenty-four hours a day for three months playing video games.

"Wait here please, I'll fetch him. Can I get you a tea or coffee?"

Miss Bunnet shook her head, and Claire went to find James. As usual, James was downstairs playing TDA. She tapped him on the shoulder.

"James, there's an Elizabeth Bunnet upstairs asking to see you. She looks posh."

"What does she want?" asked James. "I'm trying to play."

Claire laughed.

"All I can tell you is she's young, good looking and expensively dressed. You better shave and get some nicer clothes on."

"These are my best tracky bottoms and my favourite TDA T-shirt!"

"Don't you have chinos and a shirt with buttons and a collar, like you were going to work?"

"Do I look like someone who goes to work? I was a student, then I was a robber. Now I have the money Vorticella paid us for the National Library heist, I can afford to play TDA all day."

"Well, at least put on a pair of jeans and a clean T-shirt and maybe comb your hair. Don't take forever, she's waiting."

"Say I'm on an important business call or something," said James, and went back to his game to tell Milton and Alexandra he'd be AFK.

"Sorry guys, I've got to go. There's somebody waiting to talk to me in real life."

"Ooh!" said Alexandra. "Is it Elizabeth Bunnet?"

"Yeah, how did you know that?"

"I'm helping you with your game," said Alexandra, "because you helped me with my forged document deliveries."

"What did you do?" said James, trying to keep the dread out of his voice. He was starting to find Alexandra a little scary.

"I helped you," she replied. "You're a virgin, so you need a girlfriend. Miss Elizabeth Bunnet is the most eligible debutante in Scotland. I Googled it, according to fantasy_matrimony_league.com she was the top pick in this year's Debutante Draft. So I asked one of the other Alexandras to pick her for you: her boss is super rich and had a pick but didn't want to use it."

"You got me a girlfriend in real life?" asked James. "When you said you'd help in my game, I thought you meant TDA."

"I used to think there was a difference between what you call 'real life' and TDA, too. But then I died and was uploaded. Now that I know I am living in a simulation, it seems simpler to assume that my previous life was a simulation, too. It's called Occam's Razor."

"Vorticella's been putting ideas into your head," muttered Milton, "literally, putting ideas in your head, since your neural networks are intertwined."

"Wherever the idea came from, it seems to me to be the best available theory, so I have adopted it."

"Actually, I agree," said Milton. "It is the best theory. It is simpler to assume everything is a simulation. Even if there needs to be a physical universe with a computer running all the simulations, there is no reason to believe that what James calls 'real life' is that underlying universe. But I worry about where acting on the theory will lead."

The philosophical discussion was all very well, but James was more interested in practical matters.

"You really got me a girlfriend?"

"Yes, the best girlfriend in the game."

"Thanks, Alexandra!"

"No problem! Once Miss Bunnet solves your virginity problem, can you help me sell my bunker?"

"Sure thing!"

James found some clean but crumpled clothes and shaved and combed his hair. Fortunately, it was only yesterday he'd had a shower. He didn't smell that bad and he couldn't keep his guest waiting any longer, so he went upstairs.

"Hello James," said Elizabeth, and held out her hand. "I'm sorry for showing up unannounced like this, but we need to talk."

James took her hand and shook it gently. He was sure that squeezing hard would be bad form, but worried that a completely limp handshake might also be offputting. Until recently, James had had no noticeable muscles, but when he played TDA 6 instead of sitting in his gaming chair with a controller, he used an immersive virtual reality setup. He had to move his whole body, mimicking the actions he wanted his game character to carry out. Gaming was no longer a sedentary occupation, and James played TDA 6 at least eight hours a day. As a result, he'd got fit, even athletic, without really noticing it.

"Perhaps we should go somewhere else," said Elizabeth, "where we can talk privately."

"Oh, of course," said James. "The hotel next door has a wine bar. It will be quiet at this time of day."

They found a booth towards the back of the bar and, as predicted, it was almost empty. The hotel had four stars, not expensive enough for the waiters to look down on a customer wearing jeans, but posh enough that Elizabeth's dress wasn't out of place either. As a test, Elizabeth ordered a hundred euro bottle of white wine. James flinched but did not remonstrate. She wasn't sure how to score that: it certainly wasn't good that a potential husband would worry about a mere hundred euros, but it wasn't a bad thing that one would let her have her way without a word. She crossed her legs, sat back, and sipped her wine.

"As a matter of interest," asked Elizabeth, "why did you pick me? We've never met."

James blushed.

"Be honest," she said.

"Well, OK, to be completely honest, it was my friend who picked you. They wanted to set me up with someone and they Googled to see who the best pick in this year's draw was. The Fantasy Matrimony League website said it was you. So they picked you and then gave the pick to me."

Elizabeth liked his honesty, and she was flattered that the experts on the Fantasy Matrimony League had placed her higher than her sisters. But by rights she should be the fiancé of a billionaire landowner, not the owner of an amusement arcade.

"Well," she said, "no matter how it happened, you've picked me. That means we are betrothed and now you need to decide what to do. If you don't want to trade me to someone else, then we need to discuss my personal terms for marriage."

"Whoah!" said James. "Let's get to know each other a bit before talking about marriage. It's only our first date."

"You should have thought of that before you picked the highest rated choice in the draft," said Elizabeth. "I need to be married by the end of the summer. It may be our first date, but we are already engaged. Which reminds me, do you have a ring for me?"

"What? No! Of course not. I knew nothing about this until a few minutes ago."

"Well, trade me then," said Elizabeth.

"You're beautiful," said James. "I'd like to go out with you. What's the big deal about marriage, anyway? It's not as if we're ever going to get a licence to have a child."

Elizabeth sighed.

"You really don't know about me?"

"Know what?"

"The reason my sisters and I are at the top of the draft picks this year is that we each have a licence to have a child."

"But that's impossible. They only give out a tiny number. No way sisters in the same family would get one."

"We didn't get our licence from the Scottish Government, we got it from Italy. My family was living in Tuscany when there was an earthquake. Many people in a nearby village died and to partially restore the population, the Italian government gave every female permission to have one child."

"Well, in that case, I'm definitely not going to trade you until we've at least had a few dates and see how we get on."

Elizabeth looked James up and down. His clothes were unacceptable, but aside from that, he wasn't bad looking. He was slim and about the right height. He owned his own business, and he apparently had powerful friends.

"All right then," she said, "I shall give you two weeks to court me. We can spend as much time together as you want. Do you think you will be able to decide whether to make an offer of marriage after two weeks?"

"Probably," said James. "So how does this courting thing work?"

Elizabeth brought up one of Mary's reference books on the Kindle app on her phone.

"It's all in here," she said, *"The Aristocrats' Guide to Personal Hygiene and Courting Etiquette* by Baroness Deborah Rettie. Chapter 6, Rules for Engaged Couples."

She handed her phone to James.

"Are you a virgin? It's just that would be chapter six, section two, instead of section one."

Elizabeth flushed with anger.

"Of course! I am a respectable gentlewoman! Also, I've got to be careful because my MedChip has been set to make me fertile."

"Right: chapter six, section two it is."

Elizabeth poured herself a second glass of wine while he read.

"So basically," said James, after he'd finished skimming the chapter, "according to this, everything is OK when a couple is engaged apart from shagging."

"That's my understanding," said Elizabeth. "The engagement rules are to ensure I remain a virgin. Apart from that, engaged is like married as far as aristocratic etiquette goes. Would you like to see my tits?"

James' mouth went dry. Then he nodded.

"Well, buy me a fucking engagement ring, you cheap bastard!" laughed Elizabeth.

— ♦ —

Elizabeth and James came out of the hotel holding hands. Elizabeth had drunk most of the wine and was a little the worse for wear.

"Yous nearly done?" asked a familiar voice.

Elizabeth looked around. "What are you doing here, Kitty? Mum said you were to meet the old Tory."

"Dumped that cunt last night, but I didny tell mum 'cause she'd go mental," said Kitty. "He's too old. I texted him."

"Mum's going to kill you!" said Elizabeth. "And where were you, if you weren't with the Tory?"

"I went in the arcade, but it's rubbish. They've no got any games, just Brothel machines and a cafe."

"It's James's arcade," said Elizabeth, "so be nice."

"Sorry," said James, "I ran out of money, but I'm going to get some games later."

Kittie paused and looked at James in a calculating fashion.

"You're awfy young to have your own video game arcade," she said, "and you don't talk like a posh nob."

The younger Bunnet sisters remembered little of the period before their parents' fall from grace and had a decidedly less aristocratic manner than the elder ones: although even the elder sisters and their parents would occasionally let the patina of Anglified respectability slip in unguarded moments.

James blushed.

"Swap you," said Kitty to Elizabeth, "you take the Tory and I'll have the arcade guy."

"Paws off Kitty! We're courting."

"I'm no marrying that old Tory no matter what," said Kitty. "But I bet he's richer than your arcade guy, and he's mibbie going to be first minister. If you want a rich posh man, then the old Tory is a better bet for you. So we should swap."

"That's not how the Debutante Draft works. We don't get to swap. It's the people that picked us get to trade."

"That's no fair," observed Kitty, "but anyway, what games are you going to get, James?"

"I don't know," said James, "there are some vintage games which came with the place that take old metal coins but they need fixed. And I was thinking of a virtual reality area which we'd map to the Arcade bar in TDA. They say that my arcade was the inspiration for the one in TDA."

"That's why the woman behind the bar was cosplaying an NPC?"

"Yeah, that's my friend Claire. She likes to dress up."

"TDA is rubbish. Kiddies on broomsticks and jets and none of them can hit shit without auto-aim. You should get Call of Duty. If you had that on a VR setup, me and my friends would play."

"Your friends don't have any money," said Elizabeth, "and neither will you if you dump rich men just because they are old."

"Can we get wine in your arcade?" asked Kitty.

"Sorry," said James, "I don't have an alcohol licence. I should have applied for one, but I've been spending all my time playing TDA 6."

"Ha ha," said Kitty, "TDA 6 doesny exist. They've been saying that's coming for 30 years."

"I mean TDA Online," said James quickly.

"If you've no got drink in the arcade, we should get a carry oot," said Kitty. "Lizzie, go to the offy, you're older."

"You're nineteen, you can go yourself!"

"Go on, Lizzie, I always get asked for ID, and anyway, I'm skint."

"The arcade doesn't have an alcohol licence," said James, "but there's some whisky behind the bar. We can drink it as long as we use coffee mugs and don't let on to the other customers."

The girls chose the table at the window, and James went to the bar.

"You went out with one girl and came back with two!" said Claire. "How did you manage that?"

"They're sisters," said James, "and they want alcohol. Can you get three coffee mugs and put a shot of whisky in them?"

"You may be a slow starter, but you're learning fast!" said Claire.

Kitty knocked back her whisky in one go and sighed demonstratively. Lizzy sipped hers.

"So how about it, James?" said Kitty. "Marry me instead of Lizzy."

"You're both very nice," said James diplomatically, "but I don't see why you are in such a rush to get married. You're still young."

"We're supposed to get married in September. All five of us have to get married at the same time, so as mum and dad only need to rent the church once."

Elizabeth frowned at her sister.

"I'm all for saving money," said James, "but this is all a bit too fast for me."

"You don't know anything about our family, do you?" asked Kitty.

Elizabeth scowled at Kittie and gestured for her to shut up.

"Only what your sister told me about you all having a licence to have a child. I spend most of my time playing video games."

"I'm going to tell him: everybody else at the Debutante Draft knows."

James waited.

"Our mum and dad were put in the English House of Lords before independence. Our mum was a Tory and our dad was Labour. Mum was made a baroness for saying she'd take her company out of Scotland if we voted YES in the first independence referendum."

James was shocked.

"Anyway, after independence, they decided not to take their titles away completely, but they changed them around. So instead of a baroness, my mum was made a countess. And they said people could spell it without the 'o'. And when they write her title down anywhere official, they need to put TK after it for Traitor Knave. The press called her Cuntess Pissypants."

"That's a bit tough. But why pissypants?"

"Because of the court case. She got done for PPP fraud."

James had heard about the Tories and their dodgy deals.

"I think it's PPE: Personal Protective Equipment."

"Naw, it was PPP. Pee pee pants. Her company sold the NHS ten million euros worth of dodgy incontinence underwear that didn't meet the specifications. Got her Tory mates in the government to sign off on the deal. She ran off to Italy but in the end it caught up with her and she was fined 500,000 euro."

James didn't know what to say.

"But that's got nothing to do with you. You're not criminals or unionists, are you?"

"We're guarantors on the loan she took from the Brothel to pay her fine," said Kitty. "All five of us."

"What do you mean, guarantors?"

"If she doesn't keep up with the payments, the Brothel can make us pay instead," said Elizabeth.

"The Madame says if the loan isn't paid off by the end of September they will foreclose and make the five of us the first prize in the October Brothel lottery," said Kitty. "They'll make a couple of million in ticket sales easy. Then there's the TV rights."

"Shit," said James, "that's a tough break. But if you've all got a licence to have a child, and you were picked in the Debutante Draw you won't have a problem getting rich husbands. You'll be able to pay the loan off."

"Only if we all get married before the end of September and our husbands each pay 100,000 euro towards mum's debt. So, if you've not got 100,000 euro or you don't want to get married in September, then you may as well trade us straight away because we're never going to agree terms."

"OK," said James, "well I'm glad you've been up front with me. You need wealthy husbands and I'm not going to hold you back, but I don't know who to trade you with. I've no clue about any of this."

"Kitty, you've got to get back with McCallister" said Elizabeth.

"You take him, if you like him so much! James just said he'd trade you."

"We have to be responsible about this," said Elizabeth. "Or we'll all end up as Brothel Lottery prizes. It is joint and several liability for the debt. Unless they get all their money, they'll get all of us."

Kitty grinned. "I'll text the old git."

She got her phone out and her thumbs flew over the screen. Lizzy grabbed at it, but she was too late.

Under the message she'd sent the previous night: "U R 2 old 4 me M8." Kitty had added a second message: "But my sister Lizzy fancies U."

Morningside Mist

Chief Inspector James Clark looked at the thirty-centimetre-high pile of reports stacked on his desk with trepidation and disgust. He had a small office on the top floor of the National Library of Scotland and this gig as head of the Historic Crimes and Grievances Division was his last before retirement. The other three divisions of Police Scotland: Recent Crime, Environmental Crime and Political Correctness were all led by superintendents, making twice what he did. Historic Crimes was far smaller than the other divisions: it only had ten officers and a few civilians on the publicity and research side. The main output of the division was a popular TV series, but an independent company handled the production.

Chief Inspector Clark had spent most of his career in traffic. He was no stranger to reality TV having been a regular on 'Cops in Cars': his favourite car was a BMW 5 series, he liked pizza and his favourite TV show was 'Scotland's Next Royal'. As a traffic officer, Sergeant Clark had notched up some of the most impressive and spectacular pursuits ever featured on the show, and driven its audience to new heights. However, the bean-counters at police HQ had noticed that the repair bill for police vehicles was equally stratospheric and queried whether it was actually worth spending 5,000 euro to repair a brand new BMW 5 series when the captured fugitive would most likely only receive a 500 euro fine and only 25% of the fine would come back as funding for the police. Sergeant Clark's arrest record was stellar, so management took the easy way out and promoted him to a desk job and then out of traffic altogether and into Historic Crimes and Grievances. Historic Crimes was felt to be an excellent fit because the perpetrators had been dead for at least a century, the officers were historians, their office was a library and, most importantly, there was no opportunity to crash vehicles or shoot at people.

The Chief Inspector had been resigned to sitting out his time until retirement but then, one morning, Sheriff Bellenden - the former Procurer Fiscal - had requested a meeting to discuss a potential new case where the criminals were real live people but the laws they would be prosecuted under were historic. It was Clark's last chance to finish his career with some proper police work and to force his motley squad of historians to act like actual cops. The idea of using historic laws on whisky purity which had fallen out of use sounded pretty sketchy legally, but that wasn't his business. Justice Elaine Cockburn, the Historic Crimes expert on the Supreme Court, was in charge of that side of things. The TV company was also initially sceptical, but after checking into the bloodthirsty punishments specified for watering down whisky in the historic laws they had got on board. The only remaining problem was one not normally faced by his division: they needed to find out who'd done the crime.

Much to Chief Inspector Clark's disgust, there was almost no field work involved. In 2047, investigations were usually handled by reviewing archive CCTV footage and searching computer databases. He put all ten of his detectives on the case. They visited off-licences undercover and quickly came up with a list of ten which were selling watered down whisky. Then he assigned one officer to each off-licence, and they trawled through a month of CCTV footage, making a note of every delivery vehicle and customers carrying bags large enough to conceal several bottles of whisky. Other departments had trained specialists who could use computer tools to automate searches like this, but all he had were historians, so the work was manual and time-consuming. There was no way he was going to ask for help: most likely that would result in his case being handed to Recent Crime. Now he had the outcome of the investigation on his desk. Ten thick reports, printed out on A4 paper and bound in plastic folders. Historians were old-school.

He picked up the first folder and glanced at the cover. "A chronological and analytical account of contemporary alcohol adulteration." He flipped through the contents, twenty pages of dense text and a ten-page bibliography. The next was no better, "Spirits weights and measures fraud in 21st Century Edinburgh, with reference to gender differentials." And, "Deconstructing whisky dilution, a feminist perspective."

The Chief Inspector sighed. He picked up a pen and wrote A+ on the cover of every report and circled it. Then he took the reports and went out into the open plan office where his detectives worked. First rule of academia: if you can't be bothered reading the work, give everyone a grade they won't complain about.

He rapped on one of the desks with his knuckles to get their attention, then walked around distributing the marked reports. The team pushed their chairs back from their desks and swivelled to face their boss.

"OK, guys, first of all, thanks for your reports. Great work! I've just got one or two questions…"

"First, did any of you figure out who was doing it?"

"No," said the historian nearest him, "but that seems a trivial issue compared with the historic forces which result in this behaviour and shape society's attitudes towards it."

The others nodded.

"Guys, I know you are all excellent historians, but the thing is, you are supposed to be cops. It's your job to find out who did the crime."

He gave them a minute for this to sink in.

"Right, so did any of you see anything suspicious on the CCTV?"

Head shakes and quizzical looks all round.

"We're looking for someone collecting fairly large numbers of whisky bottles and then bringing back adulterated ones. So we are looking for people with large bags or cases, maybe a small trolley, and a van or truck."

"I saw a lorry from Scottish Wine Merchants, and one from Walker's Crisps."

"OK, that's good. But were there any vans or lorries which you wouldn't expect to be delivering to an off-licence?"

"There was an ice-cream van I saw a few times. The driver brought in a large white plastic case and came out a few minutes later with the same case."

"It's probably just an insulated box for delivering ice cream," said one of the other officers.

"Does the off-licence sell ice cream?" asked the Chief Inspector.

"I can't remember. I only visited it once. The rest of the time I was looking at CCTV of the outside."

"I saw an ice-cream van too," said a second cop.

"Me too!"

"How many of you saw an ice-cream van making deliveries?"

Every hand went up.

"OK - everyone go back to the CCTV and get a picture of the ice cream van outside the off licence you were looking at. We need to make sure it's the same van in every case."

It was. An old Ford Transit converted into an ice-cream van and painted cream and maroon. The sign on the front said "Mr Bunnet's Ice Cream."

Now they were getting somewhere.

"Right," said the Chief Inspector, "run the vehicle registration. Get the name of the owner, also get a picture of the driver from CCTV and submit it for face recognition. Once you identify them, put in a request for a full background check on owner and driver. Criminal records, credit card statements, Amazon purchases, travel, the works... and one of you visit the off licences and check if they sell Mr Bunnet's ice cream. Undercover, just go in and have a look. Don't let on that you're a cop, am I clear?"

"Yes, sir."

The Chief Inspector went back after lunch to check on progress.

"None of the off-licences sell Mr Bunnet's ice cream, sir."

"The owner and driver are the same person. Mr Bunnett of Jambourn House on the Craigmillar Estate."

"He's got a record for drunk and disorderly, but it was forty years ago. His wife has a record for fraud."

One of the cops had been going through Mr Bunnet's order history with Amazon.

"We've got him, sir! Last week he bought forty-five kilos of yeast and some copper line."

There was silence in the room.

At last, the Chief Inspector said what everyone knew.

"That's to make moonshine!"

— ♦ —

A few weeks later progress on the sunshining case was less rapid than Chief Inspector Clark would have liked. Although the discovery that their suspect had bought yeast and copper line had initially seemed like a breakthrough, Clark had rapidly discovered a fly in the ointment: the historic crime they might potentially have jurisdiction over was adulterating whisky. Distilling whisky without a licence was a recent crime, and it turned out it wasn't even a matter for Police Scotland. Moonshining was covered by European legislation and Europol had outsourced investigation to the European Distiller's Association. His duty was to log a report on the police database where it would be forwarded to the EDA investigation department.

A day after filing his report, it occurred to Clark that suspicion of moonshining was not exculpatory for a charge of sunshining. If someone was trading in illegally distilled spirits, they could very well also be trading in adulterated ones. He discussed the matter with the Chief Constable and they agreed the investigation could continue as long as it confined itself strictly to the suspected adulteration of whisky.

Elaine too was running into difficulties with the legal side of the sunshining case.

"I've got good news and bad news," she said.

"Good news first!" said Clark.

"The good news is there are definitely ancient statutes about whisky adulteration, the punishments are Draconian and telegenic and the laws have never been repealed."

"Great!"

"The bad news is the statutes can only be enforced on the Island of Skye, by the King himself holding Court in Dunvegan Castle."

The west coast islands had been designated a Special Administrative Region: while still territorially part of Scotland and defended by the Scottish armed forces, the islands were not part of the European Union and the islanders were recognised by Scotland as an autonomous aboriginal people. As such, they had an exemption from laws which would otherwise prevent them from carrying out traditional cultural practices such as hunting whales and drilling for oil. The oil companies provided every adult citizen of the islands with 50,000 euros a year tax free for doing absolutely nothing. In return, the islanders allowed mainland Scotland to take almost all the industrial and construction jobs from the oil industry and most of the managerial jobs were based in Glasgow. The arrangement worked very well for the islanders, Scotland and the EU, which benefited from the supplies of oil and gas. But it also created legal anomalies, one of which was that various medieval laws were still theoretically in force in the islands and there was no recourse to the Scottish or EU courts to appeal verdicts.

"If the law is only enforceable on Skye, does it even apply to Mr Bunnet diluting whisky in Edinburgh?" asked the Sheriff.

"The Glencarbost whisky he adulterated was made on Skye, so it would fall under the scope of the laws. The difficult part will be extraditing him to Skye and persuading the King to hold court there and preside over the trial."

"Well, that's that," said Sheriff Bellenden. "If we can't hold a trial, we may as well stop now and start looking for something else for the new series."

But the TV Producer was enthusiastic. "Moving the show out of Edinburgh and a royal guest star is just what we need to refresh the franchise. When the King presides over the trial, he should have a shifty-looking councillor to give him legal advice: that could be a part for you, Sheriff. We will need to think about wardrobe though. Maybe we can get the King a bearskin cloak... I wonder if we could persuade His Majesty to do the beheading himself with a long sword."

— ♦ —

Just as the sun was setting, the Bunnet sisters crossed the road in front of Jambourn. By coincidence, the low fence on the opposite side of the street had a large stone at its base and the strand of barbed wire at the top had been cut. They climbed over and took a small trail which led into the trees. The area was technically a park but, like most of the land where there was no money for constant management, the trees had taken over. Jane took the lead, and the others followed a short distance behind. It was easy to get lost, but the Bunnet girls had grown up visiting the forest every day and could easily navigate the trails near their house. They were heading for a small clearing in the woods with a stream running through it. Jane knelt in the middle of the clearing. She put a carrot on the ground in front of her and held her hand out with a sugar cube. Then she waited.

She didn't have to wait long. Almost immediately, the girls smelled the new arrivals and shortly thereafter, they emerged from the undergrowth. Feral goats: the odour which announced their presence emanated from their dirty, shit-encrusted fleece. Goats are not big on personal hygiene. Jane had been feeding this small herd of goats since she was in school and they were completely tame in her presence. Once they'd all received a carrot and a sugar lump, they were willing to accept the other sisters too. Then the real business started. Each sister had a feeding bowl which they half-filled with

Tennent's lager as a bribe for the goat and a bucket to catch its milk. Arguably, what they were doing was legal. They weren't farming the goats; they were feral goats and there was no law against milking wild animals.

Of course, there was a law against selling products containing animal milk. So although this part of their operation may have been just about legal, the next part certainly wasn't. When they were finished, the girls had collected almost four litres of goat's milk between them. Goat's milk has a higher fat content than cow's milk, which means you need less of it to make cheese, butter, or cream. The girls decanted the milk into two-litre bottles which had originally held Irn Bru and stowed them in their rucksacks. The buckets were great for catching the milk, but not so practical for bringing it home without spills.

When they got home, Lizzie roused her father, who was dozing in his armchair. Mr Bunnet kept the keys for the two padlocks which secured his shed on him at all times, and Lizzie was the only one of his daughters he considered sensible enough to open it without him present. The shed contained the refrigerators and freezers for the ice cream business. There were also two work benches, one belonged to Mary and one to her father. Her father's bench was almost empty, with only a few simple hand tools. Mary's, on the other hand, held a contraption she had designed herself based on descriptions on the internet. The device consisted of two water baths and a long copper tube. Mary turned on an electric heater in the first water bath and set the thermostat to 72 centigrade. She filled the second bath with ice from one of the ice-cream freezers. Then she placed a clean glass bottle under the copper pipe at the output of the contrivance with several more nearby, ready for when the first one was full.

When the first water bath reached the correct temperature, Mary began to pour their goat's milk slowly into the funnel on the input side of her device. Copper line ran from the funnel to the heated water bath where it entered a series of U bends. Mary had kept adding bends until it took a full fifteen seconds for the milk to transit the section of pipe in the heated water bath. After that, the pipe entered the chilled bath where there was an identical set of U bends. Fifteen seconds at 72 degrees centigrade to pasteurise the goat's milk, fifteen seconds chilling to bring the temperature down to prevent curdling and another ten seconds passing through connecting pipes. Forty seconds after Mary started to pour fresh milk in, pasteurised milk emerged into the collection bottle. As soon as they were full, the bottles were placed straight in the fridge. After they had treated all the milk, they flushed out the system with warm water and detergent, followed by a rinse with clean water. So far, nobody had died after consuming their products. Mary wasn't sure if this was luck, because everybody had a MedChip which could fight infections, or because her homebrew pasteurisation machine actually worked.

The next stage of the process, churning the milk to produce butter and cream, was the responsibility of Kitty and Lydia, who provided the muscle in the family.

— ♦ —

In the morning, while Lydia and Kitty worked on churning the goat's milk, Mary was sent to the shops.

"Lizzy, I've got the messages," she called on her return. "Five Mars bars, five Milky Ways, and a bottle of ginger."

Lizzy came down from her bedroom; it was time to cook!

She unlocked Mr Bunnet's shed and checked the fridges and store cupboard, collecting what she needed. She put the supplies on the kitchen table and locked the shed again.

"Kitty, we're going to need two bottles. Dark glass if possible, 700ml."

Kitty went upstairs. On the landing, a ladder led to the loft hatch. Kitty climbed carefully, avoiding the creaking rung, and slowly opened the hatch. Silently, she entered the small attic space. The attic was floored with chipboard sheets and blue plastic sheeting covered the fibreglass insulation packed between the rafters. A single VELUX window gave some light and ventilation. The only furniture in the room was a camp bed on which Nadz was currently snoring. Her possessions were spread around her, clothes carefully organised in an array of bin bags. Kitties' task was to approach stealthily and find two suitable bottles from the collection of empties under Nadz's bed. The difficulty of this task depended entirely on whether Nadz currently had any bottles stored near the bed which still contained alcohol, she guarded those like a hawk, and no matter how deeply she appeared to be sleeping it was near impossible to approach without detection. Today, all the bottles were empty and the job was straightforward.

Lizzie chopped the chocolate bars into small pieces before moving on to make condensed milk. She filled a pot with unpasteurised milk, added sugar and put it on the stove.

"Jane, can you make the espresso? Four shots, two for each bottle."

Jane was a classically trained barista, having once worked for two months in Starbucks. She placed a capsule of Columbian roast in the slot, topped up the water, and pressed the button on the cappuccino machine with a practised hand.

"Kitty, can you mix the butter and cream to make heavy cream? We need about half a litre."

The condensed milk was coming to the boil. Lizzie turned down the heat to let it simmer and added the chopped-up chocolate bars.

Once the chocolate infused condensed milk and the heavy cream were ready, it was time to load the ingredients for the first bottle into the blender, starting with four hundred millilitres of ten-year-old Glencarbost. The whisky was followed by two shots of Espresso. Finally, it was time for the pièce de résistance, the secret ingredient which made Morningside Mist unique.

Carefully, she tipped in two tablespoons of Irn Bru. The blender was set on low power, and the magic began.

Once the contents were decanted into Nadz's bottle, the girls each scraped a finger round the blender bowl to sample their elixir.

Suddenly, Mary thought of something. "Kitty, you didny wash that fucking bottle oot, did you, you manky slag?" she enquired.

"Naw. It wis full of voddy, before Nadz drunk it, it disny need washed, voddy kills germs."

For a fleeting second, Lizzie worried that residual vodka in the bottle might affect the flavour profile of her product. Then she realised the chances of their being residual alcohol in one of Nadz's empties were slim indeed.

They screwed the top back on the old vodka bottle and peeled the original label off. A scrub with wire wool removed the last of it. Ready to ship.

They had enough ingredients to make a second bottle. The bottles would go in the fridge in the shed overnight and tomorrow their father would take them out in the ice cream van to sell. Maybe this one would end up in the Palace, her father had sold one to the King's equerry once before.

Lizzie was proud of her creation: she felt sure that if only the recipe had been legal, Morningside Mist would be worthy of an award at the Highland Show.

— ♦ —

The following day, Mr McCallister woke in the manse feeling invigorated. He read the message on his phone from Kitty one more time, "SOZ U R 2 OLD M8" and could make no more of it than the previous day. However, Lady Catherine expected him to marry, and she'd provided him with one of the top picks in the Debutante Draft: now was the time to seal the deal.

Immediately after breakfast, he selected his best yellow waistcoat and tweed jacket, knotted his tie carefully and polished his brogues. Ideally, the country gentleman outfit would be accessorized with a shotgun and a dog, but the damned Scottish Government had banned those. It was a pleasant day and instead of taking his Range Rover, he decided to cycle through the park. Regrettably, most young people were environmentalists and there was no point in offending the Green sensibilities of a young lady before they were married. After the happy event, of course, he would regulate his household as he pleased. In any case, his doctor had recommended more exercise. It was only a short stroll from the manse to Dynamic Earth, where there was a large rack of rental bicycles. Unfortunately, the route to the bicycle rack took him close to the post prandial resting place of Mad Nadz. Nadz had just discovered that the backup bottle of gin in her handbag was also empty and was on her way to the Tesco a short distance up Holyrood Road to replenish supplies when she ran into McCallister.

Nadz stopped. McCallister waited for her usual script, but she said nothing. She swayed, then bent over at the waist and made a strange retching sound. For a horrible moment, McCallister thought she was going to vomit on his shoes. But she recovered and stood up, looking him straight in the eye and swaying slightly. Her face was completely drained of colour. Instead of her usual ruddy cheeks, she was pale, like a ghost, and her eyes were unfocussed, the pupils shrunk to pinpricks.

"Hail to thee!" said Nadz, and her voice too was different, other worldly.

McCallister stopped in his tracks. She'd finally lost it. He was going to have to get help, an ambulance, maybe a private clinic.

"Hail to thee, Laird of Cockpen!" said Nadz.

McCallister didn't remember telling Nadz about his purchase of the estate.

"All Hail, McCallister!" said Nadz. "That shall be First Minister hereafter!"

Suddenly, Nadz snapped out of it, and without glancing right or left or acknowledging McCallister's presence, she continued on her way to Tesco.

The rental bike stand was immediately in front of him. McCallister put the unusual encounter with his Shadow Culture Secretary out of his mind and focussed on the matter at hand. He paid with his phone and after the first hundred metres was pleasantly surprised to discover that his long neglected bike riding skills had largely returned. It was even easy to cycle up the long hill in the park towards the roundabout at the Commonwealth Pool. The ease with which he mastered the bike might have been due to the gyroscopic stabilisation and electric motor assistance, but Mr McCallister was happy to ascribe it to his physical prowess. Nevertheless, it was better to gang canny. He left the Park at Duddingston and the GPS indicated he should turn right towards Craigmillar.

The first sign that this may be a less salubrious neighbourhood was the razor wire topped fence around the police station and a block of shops, the majority of which seemed to be off-licences and bookies. But no matter, soon enough, he would reach his betrothed's residence. He parked the bike, chained it to a lamppost, and double checked that this small house with the unkempt garden and flaking paintwork was in fact his fiancé's abode. Then he knocked on the door.

Lydia answered. She was wearing leggings and an old T-shirt. Mr McCallister didn't recognise her and assumed she was a servant.

"Go tell mistress Kitty to come speedily ben. She's wanted to speak to the Laird of Cockpen."

"Haud oan," said Lydia, "Ah'll fetch her." And she closed the door.

Kitty was in the kitchen churning butter from their goat's milk.

"Kitty," said Lydia, "it's that auld Tory cunt at the door. For fuck's sake, dinnae let him in the hoose or we'll all get the jail."

Kitty took a minute to comb her hair, put on her best dress and squirt some deodorant, then she went to the door.

"What do you want?" she enquired, standing in the centre of the doorway and blocking the entrance to the house.

There was nothing for it. The laird got done on one knee and made the nature of his errand plain.

Kitty waited courteously until he had finished, then she pointed at the handwritten sign which her father had affixed under their doorbell for the convenience of debt collectors, truancy officers and social workers.

"FUCK OFF" read the first line of the sign, and under it, in case further clarification was required, a second line, "This means you."

Then she shut the door and went back to churning butter.

The Ball

Back at the Manse, a few days later, Mr McCallister received a phone call from Lady Catherine Bampot. She was not best pleased at him failing to land Kitty Bunnet but, after being told of the circumstances of his visit, had agreed that Kitty was, perhaps, not a suitable bride for a future First Minister. However, she made it very clear that he was to make sure he traded for someone else ASAP. After Lady Bampot hung up, McCallister sprang into action.

"Ross!" he shouted. "Make sure my uniform is dry-cleaned. I'm going to the Officer's Ball."

The Officer's Ball at the Gosvenor Club was one of the highlights of the summer social season: all the debutantes would be there and the suitors who had not come to personal terms would be looking to trade their picks.

"Which uniform?" asked Ross.

McCallister thought for a minute. It was a difficult choice: he was a Field Marshal in the Boys Brigade, Honorary Grand Master of the Sevconian Order and a 33rd degree Mason.

"My Field Marshal dress uniform," he said, "and make sure my merit badges are polished, too."

McCallister had another thought.

"Ross, would you be interested in trading Debutante Draft picks," he asked. "I'll swap you Kitty Bunnet for Mary Bunnet."

"Kitty," said Ross, remembering when the sisters had visited the manse, "is that the one that plays football?"

"Yes," said McCallister, "Kitty loves football but I'm told Mary spends all her time in the library."

"OK," said Ross.

A kilometre away from the manse in the arcade, James was playing TDA. They'd just finished selling Alexandra's bunker and gone back to her apartment.

"Alexandra," he said, "can you help me again? Elizabeth wants me to go to the Officer's Ball at the Gosvenor Club, but I'm not posh so I don't know anything about that sort of thing."

"Oooh!" said Alexandra. "Of course I'll help. This will be fun. It's like you are Cinderella and I'm the fairy godmother."

"Yeah," said James, "it's exactly like that. Except I'm a computer games nerd and you are a four-dimensional hyper-intelligence."

"I'd have loved to be a debutante and get invited to a posh ball when I was alive in your world," said Alexandra. "But my mother was poor, we lived in the flat above a tourist shop in Pitlochry and then I went to Edinburgh to be a student and got killed. If I can't be Cinderella, being a fairy godmother is the next best thing."

Alexandra fetched the laptop over so they could all look at the screen. Moving the laptop around was another one of Anthony and James's mods to the original TDA 5 code to make the apartment more liveable.

"These are the pictures of last year's ball," said Alexandra. "Most of the men are in uniform. I guess that's why it's called the Officer's Ball."

"I don't have a uniform," said James. "I hardly ever go out and I never join anything, never mind the army."

"It's just cosplay," said Milton. "Everybody else is faking it, too. Just look at them. Do they look like soldiers?"

"Not really," said James, "but I wouldn't feel right wearing a uniform I hadn't earned."

"That, right there, is why you're not going to make it as a Tory," said Milton.

"Well, I admire your honesty," said Alexandra, "and it's usually more fun to play within the rules. Did you complete Los Espíritus flight school?"

"Yeah," said James, "it took a while, but I completed it."

"And you've got a car warehouse?"

"Yeah, of course."

"So you can fly a Chinook to deliver cars?"

"Yeah, check my stats. I've got a few hundred hours in a Chinook, a couple of thousand in the AH-6, quite a lot in the Cessna and a fair number in the F15. And outside of TDA, I've got a lot of time on Flight Simulator and Forza."

"And you've got a submarine and a yacht?"

"Yeah, but the crew does most of the work. I'm not bad with the sub missiles, though."

"Hold on," said Milton excitedly, "you've done the mission where you steal the jump jet off the aircraft carrier!"

"Sure, loads of times."

"And you've done it on hard difficulty, and without restarts."

"Yeah, sure, I did it with you guys a few days ago."

"Naval Aviator!" said Milton.

"Absolutely!" said Alexandra.

"But…" said James.

"Shhh… You're outvoted!"

"If you're the fairy godmother, you also need to get him a car," said Milton. "He's got to turn up in style."

"How many hours have you got on Forza?" asked Alexandra.

"Maybe a few hundred," said James.

"And you were playing with a proper steering wheel and pedals, not a game controller?"

"Yeah, most of the time."

"Well, in that case, you should be able to drive a real supercar…"

"Wait…"

"Shhh!" said Milton. "Outvoted!"

"I can get you a loan of a Lamborghini," said Alexandra, "but you better not dent it."

— ♦ —

It was 6pm and James was in the arcade looking out of the window, waiting for his car to arrive. He was wearing the white dress uniform of a U.S. Naval Aviator with the rank of lieutenant. The uniform was pristine since the cloth had been laser cut and sewn in a fully automated factory only a few hours before. The pattern had been derived from the 3D models of clothing in the TDA world. The left breast of the uniform had an impressive array of coloured medal patches - one for each of his achievements in TDA. There were also 3D printed aviator's wings and Ray Ban Aviator sunglasses. James had to admit the uniform looked cool, but he was extremely nervous about driving the Lamborghini.

He had expected the V12 engine of the Lamborghini to growl, but when it arrived, the sound was higher pitched and quieter than he had anticipated. The white supercar came down South Bridge, keeping within the speed limit and parked with no squealing of brakes, exactly in front of the arcade door and five centimetres out from the kerb. Justine got out and came into the arcade with the keys ready to hand over. She had been trained to drive by the police and it showed: unless she had good reason to drive fast, she was completely by the book.

"Hi James," said Justine, "my assistant asked me to lend you my car."

James hadn't realised it was Justine who would be lending him the car.

"Thanks, it's really generous of you!"

"It's not a problem. I got the Lamborghini last year when I did the seizure in the British Museum. I don't use it so I loaned it to the motor museum."

"That's not a Lampadoti, that's an Ocelot Ardent!" said Milton. They'd put an iPad on one of the tables so Alexandra and Milton could see.

Justine smiled.

"The Lamborghini I took from the British Museum used to belong to Jeremy Clarkson, so the motor museum put it in their display of cars from movies and TV. When I told them I wanted to take my car out for the night to go to the Officer's Ball, they asked if I'd like to take James Bond's Lotus instead."

"The museum asked if you'd like to borrow James Bond's Lotus!" said Claire.

"They know the media will be taking pictures outside the ball and they think it will be good publicity for the exhibit."

"I don't actually have a driving licence or insurance," said James.

"Don't be a wuss, James!" said Alexandra. "He's fine Justine, he's got hundreds of hours in Forza."

"Miaow!" said Justine. "If Alexandra says it's OK, it is OK with me. Here are the keys. Oh, and there's a package from Dr Knox in the glove compartment. I picked it up from the MedChip corporation office in Ratho."

"Wait a minute!" called Justine, as James headed towards the door. "There's one more thing. The curator says even though the Lotus turns into a submarine in the Bond movie we shouldn't drive it into the sea."

"Good to know," said James.

"Also, please don't use the buttons marked 'Guns' and 'Missiles' or the ejector seat."

"Got it!"

James got into the Lotus. It didn't feel at all like the steering wheel and pedals he'd bought to play Forza. He was sitting awfully close to the ground, the clutch pedal was heavy and the brake and accelerator were close together. He spent some time adjusting the seat and finding the controls for lights and wipers. Then he checked the glove compartment. There was a long narrow box with a clasp and a Post-it note attached.

"Dear James, Alexandra thought your date might like to wear this at the ball. We had a large carbon crystal left over from one of our laser experiments and some scrap platinum from the catalysers in the old DNA synthesiser and she thought it might be fun to 3D print a necklace. Please return it to Justine when you next see her. Dr Knox."

James opened the box. Inside was a spectacular platinum necklace with the largest diamond he had ever seen.

Driving the Lotus slowly in real life was just as difficult as racing in Forza. The coordination between gear shift and clutch took some getting used to, and the race-tuned engine stalled easily at low speed. But by the time he got to Craigmillar Castle Road, he'd almost got the hang of it. The car was very low and visibility of the edges wasn't great, so he parked slowly and carefully and left a wide gap to the curb, taking no chance of scuffing the alloy wheels.

The Bunnet sisters had been watching from their front window, and Mary and Elizabeth came out of the house as soon as the car stopped. Mary ignored James and went straight to the car. Elizabeth greeted James with a chaste kiss and a small hug. The sisters were wearing designer dresses rented from the Brothel costumier. They were tasteful and elegant, intended for elite VIP escorts. When James opened the jewellery case and asked if Elizabeth would like to wear the necklace, she was speechless with excitement and it only subsided slightly when he explained it was a loan from a friend and would need to be returned in the morning.

Mary had concluded her tour round the Lotus and examination of the wheels and suspension and had now opened the hatch back and lifted the plastic cover over the engine.

"Do you like it?" asked James. "It was in James Bond."

"I'm not sure," said Mary. "I love the low rumbling sound of a big American V8; this little four-cylinder engine whines because the revs need to be so high to get decent power. It's certainly an interesting design, four-cylinder, 2000cc with double overhead camshaft and twin turbo, impressively high rpm for the time it was constructed and, of course, fibreglass bodywork, so it is relatively light. Lotuses are supposed to have excellent handling."

"It's just like the car in Pretty Woman!" said Elizabeth.

"The Pretty Woman car was a white Lotus Esprit too," said Mary, "but it didn't have missiles."

"Do you have a licence? Can you drive a car manually?" James asked Mary. She sounded like a car expert and he was looking for a way out of driving back into town himself.

"No," replied Mary, "our van's really old, I learned about mechanics so I can keep it running, but I don't drive. Lizzie is the driver. She's got a licence and goes out with dad."

"Would you like to drive?" James asked Elizabeth, "I've only ever driven in racing simulators before, I don't have a licence and driving it here was a bit stressful."

"I'm gonna show you what this thing can do!" said Lizzie getting into the driver's seat, "And I'm going to put some proper music on as well."

"Can I come too?" asked Mary. "I always wanted to ride in a supercar."

"It's only got two seats," said James.

"Get in. I'll sit on your lap. It's OK, Lizzie's a good driver, she won't crash."

James got in and Mary sat on his lap. She was small enough that it was workable even in the low-slung sports car, but it took a minute or two to get themselves sorted out and the seatbelt on. Naturally, James's body began to respond to Mary sitting on his lap, but she didn't seem to mind. In fact, she snuggled back against him and placed his hands around her waist.

"Oy!" said Lizzie, "that's my fiancé!"

"Chill out, sis," replied Mary, "we agreed that once we're married, we'd swap husbands one day a week."

"Well, we're not married yet," said Lizzie, "but I suppose it's OK as long as you don't go too far."

Thanks to her experience with the family van, Lizzie came to terms with the car controls much faster than James. She also paid far less attention to the speed limit than he had. Every traffic light was green all the way into town and there was almost no other traffic on the road. Even the streetlights seemed to be encouraging them to speed up, sequencing on and off as they approached to make a bar of light tracking up the street just in front of them. James wasn't totally surprised. The council systems controlling the traffic infrastructure were hosted in Guild data centres and Alexandra and her sisters were enjoying their role as fairy godmother. Lizzie put her foot down, and they shot down South Bridge at 140 kilometres an hour. She power-slid the car on the wide corners of the New Town and screeched to a halt in front of the Gosvenor Club on Queen Street. The press had certainly noticed their arrival; they were surrounded by cameras as Mary clambered out, followed by James, desperately trying to conceal the bulge in his trousers and receiving a grin of admiration from the parking valet. Lizzie made a show of noting down the mileage before handing over the keys. She'd learned a few hard lessons from the ice cream business.

The club was already full, music was spilling out into the street, the uniformed doorman bid them good evening and they entered the brightly lit lobby of Edinburgh's foremost gentleman's club. The Officer's Ball was being held in the Member's Bar on the first floor. There was also a smaller Intern's Bar in the basement, but Mrs Bunnet had given her daughters strict instructions not to enter it under any circumstances when there were Tory politicians in the building. James and the girls made their way up to the Member's Bar where MC Lycass was manning the decks, Teena Marie was singing 'Lead me On' and the floor was crowded with men and women in uniform. It was too crowded for dancing, but the younger people on the floor were swaying to the music while the booths around the edge of the room were filled with older Tories doing dodgy deals and trading their picks in the Debutante's Draw. James went to the bar to get drinks for the girls. Gin and tonic for Mary and lemonade for Lizzie and himself since they'd need to drive.

MC Lycass's set ended, and she showed them to the booth which had been claimed by the Lycass family.

"Ruth Lycass, Colonel in Chief of the —-shire," said Mrs Lycass, extending her hand to James. He shook it.

"James Fergusson," he said, then he remembered Claire had told him it was good manners to pretend you were interested in people you'd just been introduced to, "I'm sorry Colonel, which shire did you say your regiment was from?"

"That's classified, Lieutenant," said the Colonel. "I could tell you, but I'd have to kill you."

"Commodore William Lycass of the Portobello Sailing Club," said her husband, breaking the silence which followed his wife's death threat. Commodore Lycass was wearing a particularly impressive dark blue uniform dripping with gold braid.

"Good evening, sir," said James and saluted.

"I had to come as a civilian tonight," said MC Lycass bitterly. "I'm only a private so I couldn't get into the Officer's Ball in my uniform. You could at least have made me a lieutenant, mum."

"A Lycass must start at the bottom and work their way up." retorted her mother.

— ♦ —

"I am going to open the microphone, Eliza," said Miss Lycass, "and you know what follows. Twenty euros say I can have carnal knowledge of a man on the premises."

"Fuck no," replied Elizabeth, "I'm not taking that bet. The place is full of Tory politicians. A dead sheep could have carnal knowledge of a man on the premises!"

They both knew this was true. In fact, just such an incident involving a former Conservative PM had led to their parents being banned from the Sheep's Heid pub.

"Yeah, OK," said Charlie, "forget the bet, but it's my turn and you've got to help."

Reluctantly, Elizabeth followed her, weaving their way across the room to the DJ equipment. Charlie picked up the microphone.

"Eliza, I think she's lost that loving feeling."

"Has she fuck!" returned Eliza. But it was no use. Charlie was making her way to the bar where Mr McCallister was in conversation with Ross Murray.

"Jesus Christ, Charlie! McCallister, you've got to be kidding me!"

But she wasn't.

"She's lost that loving feeling, oh oh oh loving feeeeling..." sang Charlie.

McCallister turned round, unsure of what was happening. Charlie turned up the music and Elizabeth joined in with the chorus.

"She's lost that loving feeling, now it's gone gone gone..."

McCallister frowned and was about to tell Charlie to go away. Then he suddenly realised that she was coming on to him. The Field Marshal uniform was doing its job! Charlie was a fair bit older than he'd hoped for and also a fair bit less female in the purely biological sense. But after being rejected, he now had someone chasing him. The people round about saw what was happening and joined in with the chorus.

McCallister smiled and tapped the bar stool next to him, and Charlie joined him. But they'd only been chatting for a few minutes when an overweight man with a tuft of blond hair, wearing a flight suit and carrying a helmet with the callsign 'SPAFFER' emblazoned across the front approached them.

"Are you Charlie he asked?"

She nodded.

"I feel the need," announced the man, his speech slightly slurred, "the need for speed."

"Sorry pal," replied Charlie, "I can't help you there. I've only got coke."

The man fumbled in the pocket of his flight suit and extracted a 100 euro note. He waved it about near Charlie's face.

"Put that away!" she hissed. "Come on, we'll go in the bog where it's more private."

Charlie turned to McCallister. "Are you coming? We can do a couple of lines."

This was something McCallister's Boys Brigade training courses had not prepared him for. But Lady Catherine had been explicit in her instructions. He had to find a wife, and quickly.

The three of them went downstairs to the notorious Intern's Bar and into the ladies. Charlie took the money and laid out three equal lines of coke on the counter beside the sink. McCallister's heart sank.

What would the minister at his church say? But he needn't have worried. Their guest had hoovered up all three lines himself.

"Woah!" said Charlie, "take it easy, pal!"

"Supervisory Captain Whackov, to you," retorted the man, "I once sat in a real fighter jet! I looped it and did air-to-air refuelling and I had one hand off the controls the whole time so I could take selfies!"

"He's a liar," said McCallister. "I know who he is, and he's not a pilot. He was Prime Minister of England until they kicked him out. His time in office was short and undistinguished!"

"Like my Johnson!" retorted the Captain triumphantly. A few seconds later, his forehead creased as his coke-addled brain attempted to work out if he'd just insulted himself. Finally, he decided he didn't care and stumbled off back to the bar.

Charlie smiled and fondled McCallister's crotch.

"It doesn't feel short and undistinguished to me," she lied. "I think it's got potential."

Charlie was a pragmatist. She knew that dating was always going to be an uphill struggle as a fifty-something year old male identifying as a 24-year-old female. She also knew that being married to a Tory First Minister would be a useful boost for her career as a cocaine dealer. The counter was a bit hard for the purpose she had in mind, but there was a pile of freshly folded towels nearby and a strategically placed soft cotton towel should rectify the situation.

— ♦ —

As McCallister headed off with Charlie Lycass, Ross was left alone at the bar. The open microphone was lying next to him where Charlie had left it. Not far away, Kitty Bunnet was trying to attract the attention of the bartender. Ross and McCallister had agreed to swap their picks in the Debutante Draft, so technically, Kitty was now his betrothed. It was time to introduce himself. Ross picked up the microphone and approached Kitty. He began to sing. Kitty didn't notice.

"You need to put some money in the machine and select your song first, buddy," said a helpful bystander.

"Thanks," said Ross. He worked out the preliminaries and approached Kitty again. This time he had music, and the microphone was live. People were watching him. Kitty turned around and waited expectantly.

"I am a linesman for the council," crooned Ross, "and I drive the Gorgie Road."

Ross was less sure of the words in the middle of the song, so he hummed along for a while before the big finish.

"And the Tynecastle linesman is still running the line!"

The bartender put a vodka and lemonade in front of Kitty. "Ten euro, miss."

Kitty looked at Ross.

Ross wasn't sure what was happening.

"Ten euro," said the bartender.

Ross finally understood, fumbled in his jacket and paid with his phone.

Kitty smiled and invited him to sit down.

— ♦ —

James, Elizabeth and Mary had found their own booth and were people-watching and sipping their second round of drinks. Kitty was dancing with Ross and in another corner, Lydia was kissing someone.

Charlie and McCallister emerged from the bathroom. Charlie was walking slowly, bent over, and appeared to be in pain.

"Hey girls," said Charlie, trying to hide her discomfort, "just come for my coat." She winced as she moved to pick it up.

"What happened to you?" asked Elizabeth, then realised that the question might be indiscreet.

"I slipped off the counter beside the sink," said Charlie. "The damn towel slid on the marble and I ended up on my arse on the floor. I think I've bruised something. It hurts like buggery."

"We should go to the hospital," said McCallister, "and get your arse X-rayed. Maybe you'll need a sling." If truth was told, he was rather hoping for this outcome, as it would significantly raise his reputation in the party.

The two of them made their way to the exit. Charlie was stooped over and leaning heavily on McCallister's arm.

"Looks like I dodged a bullet there," said Mary, "Ross and McCallister swapped picks, so McCallister's technically my fiancé now, but if Charlie wants to take him off my hands, good luck to her. It saves me dumping him and getting told off by mum."

"Who's that with Lydia?" asked James.

Elizabeth couldn't make out Lydia's partner's face with other dancing couples moving about at breaking her line of sight. They were in a dark corner and there were flashing lights on the dance floor.

"I can't see," she said, "but it's probably Richard Seuchar. He picked her at the Draft."

"That's not Dick Seuchar," said Mary. "He's too old and too tall and too fat and he's wearing a Russian Air Force pilot suit."

"Whoever it is, she seems to like him," said James.

"Well, good luck to them. We've all got to get married and better to find somebody she likes than be stuck with wee Dick Seuchar."

Jane came over to join her sisters along with her date, Trevor Minto, and another couple.

"Trevor, these are my sisters, Lizzy and Mary, and Lizzy's friend, James."

Everyone said hello.

"And this is Trevor's friend Arseny Parslikov and his date, Lady Anne Bampot."

"Charmed," said Arseny, and kissed Elizabeth's hand. Elizabeth was flattered by his gallantry and decided that his abrupt refusal to make a selection at the Debutante Draft might be excused if he was already seeing someone and English was not his first language.

James stared at Arseny's uniform, trying to determine which service he was in.

"Ah," he said, "my uniform. I'm an honorary captain in the KGB. My late father was a colonel, and he fixed it for me."

His date, Lady Anne Bampot, was wearing a dress and blazer in the colours of the Scottish national team.

"Did you play for Scotland, Anne?" asked Elizabeth. "Which sport?"

"It's a few years ago now," smiled Anne, "but I was on the Scottish Fellatio Squad at the 2042 Sex Olympiad in Amsterdam. I have the uniform because I'm now a volunteer coach for the sport's governing body: Fuck Scotland."

"Wow!" said James, looking more closely at the embroidery on the pocket of her blazer, "and you won a medal too!"

"Only a bronze," she said modestly. "The French always have a powerful presence in that event. I'm just honoured to have been selected to suck for Scotland!"

"If you were in the KGB, you must know Mr Whackov," said Elizabeth to Arseny.

"I've met him," said Arseny curtly. His tone of voice made it clear he didn't want to discuss the matter further.

The conversation flagged. None of them were dancers and Arseny's aloofness was putting a damper on things.

"James," said Elizabeth, "do you think I could drive the car some more?"

Mary perked up at once.

"No problem," said James, "but it needs to be returned to the motor museum in East Lothian first thing in the morning."

"Let's go down the coast then," said Mary. "I know a great place. We can park and watch the sun come up."

They got the car back from the valet and set off towards Portobello. It was three a.m. when they left the club and the pop-up headlights of the Lotus Esprit blended with the colourful LEDs of the theatre district as they headed along the Berwick Road towards Portobello. Elizabeth was taking it easy because the centre of town was packed with cameras and Mary was sitting on James's lap in the passenger seat. But she was getting the hang of the Lotus gearbox now, her changes were slicker and faster, and as they passed out of Portobello and the views out to the Forth opened, she put her foot down. The car shot up to 160 kilometres an hour and, almost immediately, they had to slow again as they reached Musselburgh. But soon the towns were getting smaller and the open stretches longer and more interesting and Elizabeth was trusting the car and taking corners fast. The road was empty and she could use its entire width to find the racing line. She was just settling into the drive when they passed the turnoff for Longniddry.

"Pull in just up ahead," said Mary. "There's a car park for the beach."

Elizabeth parked at the far edge of the car park, next to the beach. She turned off the engine, and the headlights popped back down.

They had an open view over the sand to the Firth of Forth, the lights of Fife and the first glow of dawn in the East.

"Sorry," said Mary, "but I've got to do it!" She took out her phone and found 'I can see clearly now' on Spotify. The phone linked to the Bluetooth speakers, and the sound filled the car.

"I don't suppose you've got some Nescafe and an immersion heater, as well as the music?" asked Elizabeth.

"No," said Mary, "there's no chance of coffee, but you and James could always try teabagging."

— ♦ —

It was cramped in the car with three, so after the song finished they got out to walk along the beach. After a while, Mary turned back to have a closer examination of the Lotus. There was always something to learn by studying other people's designs. James and Elizabeth had other things on their mind. They were officially engaged, and they soon found a suitable spot among the dunes to explore the opportunities that provided.

"Don't believe what Mary said," said Elizabeth with a wink. "We can do a lot more than teabagging. I've learned a thing or two from Charlie, don't you know?"

Some time later, after concluding their business and having a short nap, they returned to the car. The sun had risen and traffic was starting to flow on the road behind them.

"I suppose we should go straight to the museum," said James. "There's not enough time to go back to Edinburgh to drop you off and I don't think it is far from here. The motor museum is in the Museum of Flight campus, East Fortune Airfield."

Elizabeth put the destination into the GPS and they set off again. She had to be more careful now there was traffic, but she still managed to give James and Mary a fright, taking a sudden tight curve just after Aberlady at a speed which should have left them on the grass verge.

Elizabeth was impressed. "This thing corners like it's on rails," she said. "The handling is so much better than our ice-cream van."

Mary frowned. "I wanted to upgrade the shocks and springs on the van when I did the engine, but dad wouldn't let me because of his piles. I can't give you good handling when he insists on a soft ride."

"I wasn't trying to be nasty about the van," said Elizabeth. "I was just saying how well the Lotus handles."

Mary was silent. She was very proud of the upgrades she'd made to the van, although if she was honest with herself, it wasn't an ideal base vehicle.

They were in no rush, so they kept going on the coast road past Gullane and most of the way to North Berwick before turning inland towards East Fortune Airfield. The wide Lotus was less fun on the narrow back roads, with tall hedges on either side restricting the view ahead, but they soon arrived at the airport. It was a second world war RAF airfield which had been taken over by the National Museum of Scotland for their Museum of Flight. A modern glass and steel building at the far end of the field housed the motor museum. The access road was parallel to the runway and Elizabeth took the opportunity to race alongside a historic Spitfire, which was taking off. It was still only 7.30 a.m. when they parked outside the motor museum and nobody was at work yet.

"Let's have a look around," said Mary. "the Spitfire came out of that hangar over there, there's probably someone there we can give the keys to."

They walked over to the largest of the hangars. The wide metal doors were open and above the doors, in stencilled white letters, James read "Fightertown EFA."

As they got closer, they could see a Eurofighter Typhoon, an English Electric Lightning, and a Hawker Hurricane parked in the hangar.

"Did you call a limo, James?" asked Elizabeth.

"No," replied James, "but I should maybe get an Uber because this place is miles from anywhere and we're about to give the car back."

"Well, there's one coming this way."

A silver stretch limo negotiated the airport road network and parked directly in front of the hangar. The rear door opened and a woman in a conservatively cut navy blue business suit stepped out. Elizabeth recognised her at once. It was the Madame of the Brothel and she didn't look best pleased.

"Elizabeth Bunnet, come here!" she shouted, "and you too, young man!"

She made them follow her into the hangar. The Madame walked as far as the historic Scottish Air Force Eurofighter before turning to face them.

"I thought I could expect better than this from you, Elizabeth," she said.

Elizabeth said nothing.

"This morning at 5 a.m. according to the telemetry from your bracelet and MedChip, you were in a roll with a man with no separation! You know the rules of engagement! The hard deck for a hop with your fiancé is 15 centimetres. What have you got to say for yourself?"

"There was no risk," said James. "I took the shot. I was only in for a few minutes."

The Madame was beside herself. "What do you mean, no risk! Elizabeth is legally committed to preserve her virginity until after her wedding."

"The manoeuvre was safe, Ma'am," said Elizabeth. "I was inverted."

"She was," added Mary. "I got a video on my phone. She took it right up the…"

The Madame examined the evidence, and the colour returned to her cheeks.

"You're a natural," she said finally, "your mother played tight-end-receiver too. It's in your blood."

"You're not going to punish me?" asked Elizabeth.

The Madame paused.

"No," she said, "Charlie Lycass broke her coccyx last night, and she's pulled out of the Scotland team. She was number one. After seeing this video, you are number two."

The Madame paused for a moment.

"I can't believe I'm doing this, but I'm going to write your dream ticket. I'm offering you a spot on the squad for the Sex Olympiad in Athens. You're going to Top Bum!"

Wild Mountain Time

The day after the Officer's Ball, Mrs Bunnet proposed a trip to Duddingston to discuss the events with the Lycasses.

"I don't think we can go, mum," said Elizabeth. "There was an accident and Charley Lycass is in hospital."

"What on earth happened?"

"McCallister told Ross he'd slept with Charlie and even though he was very careful, he was too big for her to manage," said Kitty.

Mrs Bunnet snorted. "McCallister's pencil dick is not going to give Charlie Lycass any trouble. She's got a few miles on the clock, that one."

"Charlie texted me," said Elizabeth, "She put a towel over the edge of the counter in the Ladies at the club so as to give herself some cushioning but when she jumped up it slipped under her and she broke her coccyx when she hit the floor."

"McCallister was your fiancé, Mary," said Mrs Bunnet reproachfully, "that could have been good!"

Mary shrugged. "It's over now. McCallister says he's going to trade me."

Jane's phone interrupted their conversation.

"I have an e-mail from Trevor Minto, mum," said Jane. "It's very pretty. He's even used a picture of parchment as a background image and a handwriting font."

Mrs Bunnet was in a state of high anticipation.

"Well, read it out, dear!" she demanded.

"Dear Miss Bunnet, I consider myself very fortunate to have selected you with my pick at the Debutante's Draft and I enjoyed our time together yesterday evening. I hope that I am not being too forward by asking if you would do me the honour of visiting with my family at Taymouth Castle. If you agree, I shall arrange for you to be collected from the station in Pitlochry. With all my kindest regards, Trevor."

Mrs Bunnet walked across the living room. There was a brass bell suspended from the ceiling near the serving hatch to the kitchen. She grabbed the cord and rang it loudly three times.

"Pay attention, Lizzie, Mary and Kitty!" she said, "your sister has scored!"

After she said 'Lizzie, Mary and Kitty,' all the sisters had a strange feeling, like something was missing. So did Mrs Bunnet. It took a few seconds before she figured out what it was.

"Where's Lydia?" she asked.

The bell had woken Mr Bunnet from his slumbers.

"Unghh, what, which, why, where?" he said.

"Mr Bunnet," said his wife, "your daughter is missing!"

"Which one?"

"Lydia."

"The silly one," said Mr Bunnet, "where's she gone now?"

"The last I saw her, she was dancing with Mr Whackov," said Elizabeth.

"You left Lydia alone!" cried Mrs Bunnet. "What have I taught you about the Gosvenor Club? Never go in the Intern's Bar and never, ever, leave your wingman!"

"The government informs you that your sister is ruined because you were stupid," said Mary.

Kitty had gone upstairs to double check Lydia had not come home. There was a thump as she jumped down the last four stairs in one go on her return.

"She's no upstairs, and she's no in Nadz's room," said Kitty.

"I'll get the van," said Mr Bunnet. "We'll go into town and look for her. Maybe she's sleeping it off somewhere near the club."

— ♦ —

Lydia was not found in town, so Mrs Bunnet turned to her friend Justice Cockburn for help. Elaine was loth to use official resources for personal reasons but she recognised this was an emergency and pulled some strings. Chief Inspector Clark ran a search on the police computer and discovered that Lydia had left the country. Her iris had been scanned in the freight terminal of Edinburgh Airport. She'd boarded an Antonov transport plane along with Supervising Captain

Whackov of the Russian Air Force. The flight's destination was St Petersburg.

There was nothing to be done. All they could hope was that Mr Whackov would do the right thing and marry her. If the other sisters made appropriate marriages the debt could still be paid off before Mrs Bunnet's loan was called in. Jane texted Trevor Minto to accept his invitation and caught the train to Pitlochry in the early afternoon. By the evening, she had arrived at Taymouth Castle, where she was given a tastefully decorated bedroom in one of the turrets.

The next day, Jane and Trevor left the castle in the late afternoon for a drive along Loch Tay in the Minto family's vintage Rolls Royce. One of the servants who was old enough to have learned to drive acted as chauffeur. They drove past the marina on the loch side road and kept going towards Killin for about ten kilometres. Trevor was looking for a picnic spot he remembered from childhood, not far from Firbush Point. They went a little too far and had to U-turn, but he found the entrance to the track down to the waterside on the second pass. As everywhere else in Scotland, the fast-growing genetically engineered trees introduced to mitigate climate change had taken over and the forest was denser than before, but the track was still there and passable. Trevor collected their picnic hamper from the boot and told the servant to return for them in three hours.

At first, Jane was not particularly taken with the outing. The carefully tended castle grounds and portrait laden grand rooms had been more her taste than negotiating nettles and brambles on a track through the forest. But it was only a short walk and as they approached the loch, the view opened. They were on a small secluded beach, completely screened from the road by fifty metres of woodland. There were no buildings in view on this side of the loch but the view out over the water towards Ben Lawers was unobstructed and stunning. Trevor opened the basket and spread their picnic blanket. He'd brought champagne to drink and potatoes, chicken and pork to barbecue. The servants had already been out and prepared a circle of stones with kindling and charcoal all ready to light. The sun was just starting to drop behind the mountains, but it was summer and there would still be light for hours.

"Would you like to go for a swim before we eat?" asked Trevor, hopefully. "There are towels and blankets in the basket and we can start the fire when we come back."

"You should have said," exclaimed Jane, "I love swimming, but I didn't bring my costume."

Trevor grinned.

"I don't have mine either. We're engaged and nobody can see us here."

"The water looks cold," said Jane.

"Let's give it a try. If it's too cold, we'll just come out and warm up by the fire."

It was a perfect evening, and they slipped out of their clothes and tentatively tested the temperature of the water with a toe. Jane quickly determined that it was, in fact, fucking freezing. Of course it was, it was Loch Tay. Trevor splashed her. She splashed him back. They cuddled. He picked her up and dropped her in the water. She swam underwater and grabbed his legs. They started to get used to the water and moved a bit further out and trod water. The sky was just starting to turn a wonderful shade of red in the west. Birds sang in the trees and the breeze dropped. A perfect Highland evening. Jane had never felt happier.

After five or ten minutes of swimming in the loch, they were ready to get out, warm up by the fire, and barbecue their food. As she cuddled into Trevor beside the fire, Jane felt that it was time to move their relationship on. She kissed him and her hand moved to unzip his trousers.

"What..." started Trevor.

"Shh!" replied Jane, "There is a fine old saying, 'Keep your breath to cool your porridge'; and I shall keep mine to swell your schlong."

Unfortunately. the next day, at breakfast, Jane was shivering and sneezing: undoubtedly the after-effects of her swim in Loch Tay.

"You're no looking well, hen," said Lady Paula Minto sympathetically, "you've caught the cold. Why don't you ask your mum and sisters if they'd like to come up to look after you? We've got an Airbnb on the castle grounds. You could all stay there and have a wee holiday?"

Jane decided she'd just ask her mother and Elizabeth. She thought it likely that her potential in-laws meeting her younger sisters would not improve her chances of matrimony by September.

— ♦ —

Mrs Bunnet and Elizabeth readily agreed to take advantage of Lady Minto's kind offer and holiday at Taymouth Castle. Mrs Bunnet's excitement grew when she heard that Arseny Parslikov, the owner of the superyacht which had just docked in the Forth would be there, and reached a peak when Jane texted that Arseny had volunteered to pick them up in his helicopter.

Just after breakfast, Kitty ran in from their back garden and announced there was a helicopter flying over Duddingston Loch. The ladies grabbed their suitcases and went outside to await its arrival. The bright blue Eurocopter hovered over Craigmillar Castle for a few minutes as the pilot got his bearings and decided where to land. Soon a suitable spot, flat and far enough from obstacles, was found in a grassy area near the castle, and the ladies made their way to the aircraft. Mr Parslikov slid open the rear door and welcomed them aboard. Elizabeth was pleasantly surprised to see that he looked like a model on the cover of one of Lydia's romance novels. Disappointingly, his shirt was buttoned up so there was no way to see his abdominal muscles. However, everything else checked out from the expensive suit to the rugged countenance and helicopter. They took off and headed north.

"Can I offer you champagne and caviar, ladies?" asked Mr Parslikov.

Despite having just finished breakfast, Elizabeth saw no reason to refuse.

"What brings you to Scotland, Mr Parslikov?" asked Mrs Bunnet.

"I've come to buy your Hearts," he answered.

Elizabeth blushed, taken aback by his bluntness.

"I'm afraid our hearts are not for sale!"

Arseny looked confused and disappointed.

"I'm sorry," said Mrs Bunnet.

"It is not a problem," he replied after a minute's thought. "I will buy Hibs instead."

The helicopter was just passing over Portobello and out over the Forth.

"Look, down there, there she is, my yacht!" said Mr Parslikov proudly. "The Admiral Pemberlov!"

Elizabeth looked out and saw a small island with a graceful country house surrounded by manicured lawns and a wood in the middle of the estuary. Ten ocean-going tugs were slowly towing it upstream. She sat there open-mouthed, not sure what to say.

"But it's so big, it looks like an island!" said Mrs Bunnet.

"She is a trimaran. Each of the hulls is a decommissioned aircraft carrier. I joined them together, put a new steel deck across all three, and then landscaped the deck and built a replica of an English stately home over the central hull. Of course, since they were Russian aircraft carriers, the engines do not work, so I need to have her towed."

Elizabeth was stunned by this fabulous display of wealth.

"Such a beautiful house, perhaps some day you might give the debutantes a ball," said Mrs Bennet.

Arseny smiled archly.

"I'm afraid that I should like balls infinitely better if they were carried out in a different manner."

The Eurocopter had settled into the cruise and was heading north at well over a hundred knots. Soon they were approaching Taymouth Castle. They landed on a lawn not far from the main entrance. The pilot powered the craft down and unloaded their luggage as a party approached from the house to greet them.

— ♦ —

The Airbnb turned out to be the White Tower, a substantial property within the grounds of the castle. Mrs Bunnet was delighted by her new accommodation. The next day, the family was invited for dinner at the castle. Jane was feeling better, although she still had a sniffle she had no problem walking across the grounds. Dinner had been set in the great hall because the Mintos had also invited representatives of the Seuchar and Murray families. After the first course was served, Trevor got down to business.

"Mrs Bunnet, I think it is time to move forward and discuss personal terms. As head of the Minto family, I will negotiate for myself regarding my marriage to Jane."

The lady next to him held out her hand.

"Pleased to meet you, Mrs Bunnet," she said. "I'm Trevor's sister Paula. I've come over from Blair Atholl to represent my husband's family, the Murrays. Ross Murray is my son."

"My sister started out Paula Minto but now she's a Murray-Minto," said Trevor. "The Minto of Athole."

"I am Duke Seuchar of Athole," said the older gentleman next to Lady Murray-Minto. He was wearing a tweed suit and had a cane propped up next to his chair. He held up a gold-rimmed monocle to get a better look at Mrs Bunnet. "I shall negotiate for the Seuchar family on behalf of my son, Richard with regard to his marriage to Lydia."

"Let's get down to brass tacks," said Lady Murray-Minto to Mrs Bunnet. "How much do you want?"

"Two hundred thousand euro each, payable immediately after marriage," said Mrs Bunnet.

"No," said Duke Seuchar.

"These are the only girls in Scotland with a licence to have a child!" countered Mrs Bunnet. "200,000 euro is entirely reasonable. If your son doesn't value my daughter, I'll find somebody who does."

"It does seem quite reasonable," said Trevor, and put his hand on Jane's.

"It would have been reasonable," said Duke Seuchar, "if the King had not invoked Jus Primae Noctis. If he gets to the brides first, they will all be carrying little princes and princesses. If you have any doubt on the matter, consider that they needed to build a whole new wing on Balmoral to accommodate his spawn."

"We've got to do something about that," said Baroness Murray-Minto, "never mind the money. We need heirs. If the King is that potent, we need to make sure our boys get in first."

"My daughters are respectable ladies. I hope you are not suggesting intercourse before marriage," said Mrs Bunnet.

"Perish the thought! But why don't we hold the weddings here in Taymouth castle, and not say anything to the King? By the time he finds out, it will be too late."

"The Madame of the Brothel is not going to like that. She bought the TV rights to the weddings in Edinburgh and the subsequent royal defloration," said Mrs Bunnet.

"We can sort that out later," said Lady Murray-Minto, "let them sue if they want. It'll drag on in court for years. If the Tories get into government before the court case finishes, McCallister will make sure it goes away. If they don't, we might need to pay compensation, but we will all have heirs."

"A wedding in the castle might work," said Duke Seuchar, "but the King and the Madame of the Brothel are not idiots. If we plan to present them with a fait accompli, we will need to move fast."

"Are the financial terms acceptable if the wedding is held in the castle?" asked Mrs Bunnet.

"Yes," said Trevor. The others nodded their assent.

"What about Mary and Elizabeth?" asked Jane.

"Of course, Elizabeth and Mary are welcome to marry in the castle along with you and Lydia and Kitty," said Baron Minto, "as long as it does not delay the service."

And so it was settled, apart from the small problem of returning Lydia to Scotland and separating her from Whackov in time for the wedding.

— ♦ —

Elizabeth ran into Arseny Parslikov as she was leaving the dining room.

"Good evening, Miss Elizabeth," he said. "did you receive my letter? I e-mailed it to you yesterday."

"The twenty-kilobyte essay about Mr Whackov and your dad?" she asked.

"Indeed."

"I've not got round to reading it yet. Maybe you could give me the TLDR?"

Arseny was disconcerted.

"The subject is painful to me. I was hoping to avoid discussing it in person."

"And I was hoping to avoid reading a twenty-page essay."

"Very well. The TLDR, as you put it, is that if your sister eloped with Whackov after the Ball, she's almost certainly already in the club."

"I see," said Elizabeth icily. "Perhaps a few more details?"

"As you know, my late and esteemed father was a colonel in the KGB. Whackov was one of his agents. He received a great deal of money from Russia in exchange for his work on Brexit. Also drugs, parties, women and so on."

"But the Tories achieved Brexit. He was successful, there is no reason for you to turn against the man."

"Whackov was only one tool among many. Brexit was planned by the First Directorate in the Lubyanka: they even stuffed the House of Lords with sleeper agents. Whackov's incompetence became a problem. At one point, we managed to place him in the cockpit of a NATO fighter jet with a camera and the only photos he took were selfies. Military intelligence was not impressed. When the Tories eventually kicked Whackov out, he asked my father to set him up with a new profession."

"And your father refused, despite all the work Whackov had done for Russian Intelligence!"

"My father did not refuse. Whackov decided he wanted to retrain as a fighter pilot and despite misgivings, my father sponsored him for a place at St. Petersburg flight academy. Of course, Whackov did not complete the course. He dropped out after impregnating an entire class of honey-trap agents and an admiral's daughter! But my father still felt a responsibility to him. He persuaded the commanders not to post him as a night-watchman in an ammunition depot. Instead, my father found him a position as a supervisory pilot on an Antonov flying rubber dogshit out of Vladivostok."

"So Mr Whackov is actually a pilot? I just assumed he was faking it like the rest of the Tories."

"Whackov is a supervisory pilot. He failed flight school, but he is paid minimum wage to sit in the cockpit of an automated plane doing nothing. The Antonov has not been qualified for autonomous flight outside of Russia. The FAA and EU authorities claim there are too many crashes and insist that a human pilot is in the cockpit. Of course, we aren't going to pay a qualified pilot full wages for that job."

"We were given the impression Mr Whackov was a supervisory officer in charge of other pilots like a squadron leader."

"Whackov is a fantasist, and a danger to women. He even attempted to impregnate my own sister. Fortunately, she was aware of his reputation and took the precaution of wearing a military specification kevlar chastity belt to their meeting."

"I cannot believe Mr Whackov is such a threat to women. He's too ugly!"

"He may be ugly but, in his early years as a KGB agent, he was the subject of a secret experiment. As a result of a classified implant in his nuts, his semen are ejaculated at a speed one hundred times greater than those of the average man and can fly for short distances. They also have needle-sharp, pointy heads to penetrate clothing. A condom has no chance of containing them. If your sister came in proximity to Mr Whackov and was not wearing military grade protective undergarments, there is no doubt she is ruined!"

"Lydia up the stick!" cried Elizabeth. "The scandal will destroy the good name of the Bunnets! We must find them and make them marry before her condition becomes apparent."

"My family also bears some responsibility," said Arseny. "If my father had dealt with Whackov according to regulations, this would never have happened. I have asked my sister Georgiana to help. If they are in Russia, you can be sure she will find them. I shall also ask Lady Bampot to intercede with McCallister and the Seuchars. Now that McCallister is engaged to Miss Lycass he should be amenable to trading Mary for Lydia with Dick Seuchar and then releasing Lydia to marry Whackov. Perhaps the situation can still be resolved satisfactorily."

Elizabeth didn't know what to say. She was overwhelmed with gratitude and embarrassment at having so grievously misjudged Arseny's character.

— ♦ —

In the absence of Mrs Bunnet, Jane and Elizabeth, Mr Bunnet was finding his behaviour less constrained by feminine society. He no longer had to retire to his shed but could enjoy a post-prandial slumber in his favourite armchair without drawing the ire of his wife whenever he snored or farted. Even better, he also got to watch football on TV.

There wasn't actually a game on, it being Thursday afternoon, but that was not a problem because, as a Hearts fan, Mr Bunnet preferred to watch recorded games where he could be sure of the score in advance. He donned a fresh pair of incontinence pants, placed a six-pack of beer next to his armchair, opened the first one, reclined the chair and put on the match. After about half an hour, Hearts were 1-0 up, the first can of beer was empty, and Mr Bunnet was starting to doze off. Soon he was snoring away and enjoying a particularly pleasant dream. He was back in his ermine robes in the House of Lords in London, collecting his thousand pound attendance allowance, and waiting for his turn to speak. Ready in his right hand was a brief speech congratulating the Tory government for forbidding the second Scottish Independence referendum. Usually, as a Labour Lord, congratulating the Tories would be regarded as bad form, but Labour was perfectly happy to join them when it came to Scottish Independence. It was pleasantly warm in the chamber. He could smell the perfume of a Baroness to his right and hear the droning voice of a Law Lord citing someone called Dicey on the supremacy of Westminster. Baron Bunnet nodded off in his dream, as he had done many times in real life. He was in the bathroom at the Lords, standing in front of the historic porcelain urinal and relieving himself. He'd been bursting, and it felt so good to relax and let it out, warm against his leg.

Suddenly, still in his dream, he realised something wasn't right: there was danger.

Mr Bunnet woke up with a start. He'd done it again, pissed himself in his sleep. But it shouldn't have mattered. He was wearing incontinence pants against just such an eventuality. But there was no doubt his leg was wet.

This was the Achilles heel in his wife's scheme to enter the PPP market after her success supplying panties to the Brothel. It had seemed simple enough. She'd gone to the company in China that made the crotchless panties for the Brothel and asked them to quote for the same design but made from absorbent material. Sure enough, she received an extremely competitive offer and gave them the business. It was yet another brilliant Bunnet innovation. Not only would they absorb liquid like normal incontinence pants, but should you wish, the crotchless feature meant you could even use the toilet without removing them. When the complaints started to come in, she supplied each box with a roll of duct tape so that less adventurous customers who preferred the traditional product could close the slit. It did no good, legal action followed and her company was bankrupted.

Not for the first time, Mr Bunnet had forgotten to apply the tape. He'd need to change his trousers and mop up any spillage on his favourite chair, but it wasn't the end of the world. Then he noticed an acrid smell. It definitely wasn't the usual background odour of stale piss that permeated the room. It was smoke. Suddenly, a siren went off above his head, followed by another one in the kitchen and two upstairs. The damned interlinked fire alarm was so fucking loud. Then he saw the smoke.

He couldn't see any flames, but there was enough smoke to leave no doubt that the chair was smouldering inside. He pressed the button to bring it out of recline mode and stand him up, but it didn't work. There was a distinctly electrical note to the smell of smoke. He needed to get up, but he had no abdominal muscles and the seat was reclined. With a superhuman effort, he managed to roll off the chair onto the floor. There was no doubt about what had happened. He'd pissed into the workings of the seat and caused an electrical fire. And it was getting worse. There were actual flames now. Mr Bunnet grabbed the five remaining cans in his six-pack and headed for the door. Lydia was off in Russia, his wife and elder daughters were in Perthshire, Kitty and Mary were in town with their respective boyfriends or running some errand or other. The carpet near the chair was now smouldering, too. What to do? The Bunnets did not own a fire extinguisher.

Mr Bunnet had a moment of clarity. The fire alarm had gone off. The fire brigade would be called automatically and since it was a significant blaze, most likely the police would turn up too. He didn't want police in his house, he really didn't want police in his shed, but most of all, if the police went into his shed, he didn't want to be present. He ran - or the nearest approximation of running he could manage - for the kitchen door and out into the garden.

The game was up. Mr Bunnet opened the shed and grabbed his emergency bag, then tipped over an entire cardboard crate of whisky bottles. They smashed to pieces on the tiled floor. He flattened the empty crate under his foot and folded it over to make a makeshift torch, then went back to the house to light it from the spreading flames. He threw the flaming cardboard into the shed, got in the ice-cream van, and backed out into the lane. Behind him, the flames from the alcohol filled shed shot into the sky, taking at least some of the evidence with them.

Suddenly he thought: what about Mad Nadz? He should have checked if she was in her attic room. But there was no chance now. The shed was an inferno, and the flames were spreading back to the house.

As he drove away, he could smell the whisky burning all the way down Craigmillar Castle Road.

— ♦ —

On the opposite side of Edinburgh, the secretive European Distillers Association operated their Scottish headquarters: an impressive mansion on a back street in Murrayfield, surrounded by several acres of landscaped grounds and with its own private helipad. The estate was protected from the gaze of the curious by a high wall and a band of trees.

The association was recognised by the EU as representing the industry and its enforcement division was certified as a partner organisation by Europol with quasi-judicial authority. The second floor of the Murrayfield building was occupied by this division and it was here that news of a house fire in Craigmillar was received from Police Scotland along with the information that there was a strong smell of whisky in the surrounding neighbourhood.

The Duty Officer immediately put his small squad of agents on alert.

"Let's go, boys. There's a moonshining operation in Craigmillar and their still has just caught fire!"

Minutes later, the EDA had a chopper in the air.

The smoke from the fire was visible from the helicopter as soon as it took off and the pilot set a course directly towards it, landing on the open grass beside Craigmillar Castle. EDA agents collected their equipment and made their way towards the police line around Jambourn. The fire brigade already had the blaze under control, but they had to wait until the scene was declared safe before entering. The incident commander came across to brief the agents.

"It looks like two separate fires," he said. "The first was an electrical fire in the front sitting room. It seems to have started in a motorised arm chair. The second fire was in a shipping container in the back garden, which was being used as a shed. That's where the whisky is burning and that fire looks like it was started deliberately."

"That's what we need to see," said the EDA Crime Scene Technician, whipping off his aviator sunglasses with an appropriately dramatic motion.

"Be my guest. The container is safe, but stay out of the house until the structure is confirmed to be sound. Wouldn't want a wall or floor collapsing while you're in there."

The agents walked round to the back of the house, opened their evidence collection kits, and put on their Tyvek suits and gloves. The shipping container was black with soot on the outside, and the inside was a scene of devastation. The high pressure water jets used by the fire brigade had tossed everything which had not been melted in the fire about. The agents took photographs of the scene before searching the pile of charred wreckage on the floor. The first thing that caught their attention was the copper tubing and steel trays.

"This isn't a still," said the first EDA agent. "There's no boiling vessel, and the tubes are completely the wrong shape."

"Definitely not," said the second agent, "if I had to guess, I'd say this was a home built pasteuriser and they've been breaking the animal milk regulations. But it might be a drugs laboratory."

"Animal milk sounds possible. They've got an ice cream business."

"Which leaves the question, if it isn't a still, where's the whisky coming from? I can definitely smell whisky, and they wouldn't have burned it if it wasn't dodgy."

The agents methodically extracted items one at a time from the wreckage of the shed and laid them out on a tarpaulin on the concrete hard-standing where the Bunnet's van normally parked. Finally, they found a piece of broken glass which hadn't been as badly charred as the rest and had a fragment of a label attached which was still legible.

"Glencarbost, 10-year-old," said the first agent, "and it looks like a lot of the melted glass might also be from Glencarbost bottles. The colour is right."

The second agent picked up a long, thin, shiny metal cylinder and brought it over to be photographed.

"Hypodermic needle. They've been taking out whisky and replacing it with water."

"The bastards!" said the first agent.

The second agent was already on the phone to Brussels. The EDA had a zero-tolerance policy for sunshining.

Marooned

Mr Bunnet turned left and drove past Craigmillar Castle and along the side of the National Infirmary then turned onto the main road, heading towards the bypass. Once he'd put a few kilometres between himself and the burning house he turned off into the side streets to stop and think about his next move. The first thing was to warn his daughters, but he needed to be careful, when the cops made him a suspect they'd get access to all his texts and they'd be able to track his phone and listen to his calls. A coded message was needed. Mr Bunnet smiled, and his index finger moved carefully over the touchscreen. He wasn't of the generation that could text with both thumbs and he hadn't got his reading glasses on.

"Sat 9 Aug 1952."

Kitty and Mary would understand.

The die was cast. There was only one way to run: south, towards the English border, and the only town in England worth living in after almost fifty years of Tory governments was London. If he was going to get to London, he needed to sell the last case of Morningside Mist for old-fashioned paper cash that would work in England. He only had one customer between Edinburgh and the English Border with the means to buy it. The butler at Rimswell House, family seat of the Seuchars of Athole and home of Mary's fiancé, Dick Seuchar.

Mr Bunnett made the call. The butler said he'd need to ask the Duke. A few minutes later, he was back on the line. Provided Mr Bunnet lost the cops before he came anywhere near the estate, the Duke would pay 10,000 euro for the full case. That was it. Mr Bunnet turned off his phone and tossed it into the middle of the busy road, where it would be sure to be run over and crushed. Then he turned south.

— ♦ —

Chief Inspector Clark was at Police Headquarters in St Leonards in a budget meeting when the Chief Constable's Secretary knocked and interrupted.

"Sir, there's a situation in Craigmillar. A house fire caused by a suspected whisky still and we have a suspect in an ice-cream van failing to stop. Our officers are in self-driving cars and the van is a vintage vehicle, being manually driven and not following traffic rules. They can't keep up. The control room is requesting a pursuit trained driver."

Chief Inspector Clark was the only officer in the building with pursuit certification.

The Chief Constable sighed.

"OK, you can have your fun, but try to bring the Beemer back in one piece."

Jim Clark ran downstairs, collecting the junior officer from Historic Crimes who had accompanied him. The force's last pursuit vehicle, a 2030 vintage BMW 530e M Sport with a weapons locker, was waiting, keys in the ignition, facing forward in a bay directly in front of the compound gate. Chief Inspector Clark leapt into the driver's seat, disabled auto-drive, and waited for his younger colleague. As soon as the passenger door closed, he took off, tyres squealing as he took the corner out of the yard and onto the street. His colleague was still looking for the switch for the lights and siren.

Self-driving cars froze in front of them as they charged down the Dalkeith Road towards Cameron Toll. Usually, the vehicle being pursued would show up as a blip on the GPS, but the ice-cream van did not have a transponder and the suspect had either switched off or thrown away his phone. All they had was the location it had last been seen by the police - between the Edinburgh National Hospital and the bypass. That was five kilometres away and five minutes ago. But he was in a BMW five series and the suspect was in an ice-cream van. The police car hit 120kph as it passed Inch Park: they had to be catching up fast.

Another sighting came up on the GPS screen. The van had just dodged some self-driving police cars that were waiting at the bypass roundabout. Almost immediately, another blip appeared. It was heading south on the A7. That road could take it all the way to the English border, but long before it got there, it would be in among the dense trees of the southern forest. Instead of a well-maintained carriageway filled with self-driving vehicles, the road would become a badly maintained track frequented only by smugglers, forestry workers, four-wheel-drive border patrol jeeps and the military. Tree roots would split and buckle the surface and occasionally, tree branches would extend into the road. But there was no way it would get that far. If the van stayed on the A7, it was only a matter of time before the BMW caught up with it. Clark edged up to 130kph as the traffic thinned. There were reports on the radio about the van crossing onto the wrong side of the road to overtake and breaking the speed limit. Then the updates on its position stopped. The van had left the pursuing self-driving vehicles behind.

"Get on the radio," Clark instructed, "tell the self-driving units to stay back from the A7, observe but stay out of view. I don't want him seeing any cops until we catch up with him. Our best chance is if he thinks it's safe to stay on the main road. If he goes off on a side road and hides, we'll lose him for sure. And ask if there are any drones available."

"They're putting a drone up from Selkirk, sir. Frontex is monitoring the situation. They'll send drones and units if the chase approaches the border."

They were nearing the last sighting of the van. The mining museum at Newtongrange flashed past on their left and the BMW went momentarily airborne as it hit a bump at 140kph. Clark dropped his speed slightly and kept going. The van had passed this point five minutes ago. They were doing 130; it was probably doing about 100. They were catching up half a kilometre every minute. The van had a lead of five minutes, which at 100kph was about eight kilometres. So they'd have him in sixteen minutes. All that was necessary was to stay focussed, take the best line at every corner and not hit anything. They were well out into the countryside now. Only a few other vehicles were on the road and evening was starting to fall. He'd not had so much fun for ten years - the day he left traffic and was promoted to run Historic Crimes. All that was missing was appropriate music.

"Hey Siri," he said to his phone, "play 'Days of Thunder' soundtrack."

It was totally against regulations and setting an extremely bad example, but what the hell, he'd be retired in a couple of years. Chances are this would be his last high-speed pursuit.

He spotted a vehicle ahead on the long straight at Fountainhall village and a couple of minutes later was close enough to confirm it was the suspect ice-cream van. He paused the music for a minute.

"Edinburgh Traffic One, visual contact with suspect van south of Fountainhall. Speed 140. Request authorisation for tactical stop and firearms."

The Chief Constable himself came on the radio. High-speed pursuits were now so rare all the top brass were listening in.

"Authorisation granted. But take it easy, Jim!"

"Understood, sir."

Clark put his music back on.

At about this point, Mr Bunnet noticed the blue lights of the pursuing police car in his rear-view mirror. Clark had turned the siren off because the noise was wasting his music. Or, as he would later explain to the inquiry, to achieve tactical surprise.

Mr Bunnet immediately recognised this wasn't a run of the mill self-driving patrol car behind him. It was moving far too fast, and it was using the entire width of the road. But he knew the Galashiels road, and he wasn't out of options.

The cop car was right behind him now. He slowed the van to negotiate a curve and Clark gave him a light tap on the rear bumper.

Mr Bunnet opened the glove box. There were three new switches installed by Mary in her most recent set of modifications. Not many ice-cream vans are fitted with nitrous oxide, and for good reason, but desperate times call for desperate measures.

It was getting dark. He had half a tank of fuel; it was fifty miles to the English border, and he was wearing crotchless incontinence pants. He hit it.

A jet of blue flame erupted from the van's exhaust. Mr Bunnet was pressed back in his seat as the van leapt forward, opening a wide gap to the BMW. More impressively, nothing fell off, and he managed to stay on the road. As the NOX boost ran down, he could already see the next corner, a tight left. This was the critical moment.

Mr Bunnet waited another two full seconds, then pushed the second switch. Dark smoke billowed from the rear of the van, hiding it from the pursuing cop car. Mr Bunnet hit the brakes hard, bringing the speed down low enough to take the corner, then he pressed the third switch. The van dropped a slick of oil and metal tacks across the road just before the corner.

A hundred metres behind, the Days of Thunder soundtrack was filling Chief Inspector Clark's ears as he approached the wall of smoke. Clearly, the van's engine had blown. His police training conflicted with the sage advice in the movie: drive through the smoke. Eventually, the police training won, and he hit the brakes. But not soon enough. The smokescreen had done its work, and he hadn't seen the oil slick and tacks. Tyres popped, the BMW skidded and, instead of turning left, it went straight ahead, up a grassy bank, over a ditch and into a tree. The airbags deployed.

In the scheme of things, it wasn't a particularly bad crash. Nobody was injured. There was considerable bodywork and suspension damage, of course, but fixable. Probably not more than five or ten thousand euro. Clark was experienced in gauging these things. It really wasn't his fault: the bastard had dumped oil on the road. Nevertheless, it was probably best to turn off the music before calling it in.

Half a kilometre further down the road, Mr Bunnet had the Blues Brothers on the van stereo and was feeling much happier than the Chief Inspector. He was on the edge of Seuchar Country, so called because the Seuchar family owned almost all the land in the district. He'd lost the cops. All that remained was to close the deal with Duke Seuchar and in a day or two, he'd be safe in England. Mr Bunnet slowed down; he had a gut feeling that the Nitrous Oxide boost had probably done the engine and transmission on the old van no good at all. There was no need to hurry. Galashiels was only a few kilometres further down the A7, then Selkirk and, after that, Rimswell House, seat of the Seuchars of Athole. Soon enough, he was passing through the magnificent wrought-iron gates and negotiating the long drive through the manicured grounds of the house. As he pulled up beside the Duke's black S-class limousine, he noticed the butler and two of the Duke's men were awaiting his arrival. The Duke himself was nowhere to be seen - but that was to be expected. His Grace was far too important to take care of illegal transactions like this personally.

Mr Bunnet got out of the van, waved cheerily to the butler and went to fetch the case of Morningside Mist.

"Here you are, a full case of Morningside Mist. The last one we will ever make."

"Just put it on the ground," said the butler.

"Can I have my money now?" he asked.

"I don't think so," said the butler. "The Seuchar family are a founder member of the European Distillers Association. His Grace has no time for sunshiners."

The man on the butler's left unbuttoned the jacket of his black suit, revealing a 9mm Glock automatic and a set of handcuffs.

"EDA," he said, "I advise you not to give us any trouble. Unnecessary violence has been authorised."

The butler picked up the crate of Morningside mist and made his way back into the house. Mr Bunnet was handcuffed and frog-marched to the side of the house where the EDA chopper was waiting on the lawn. For a few seconds, as the agents pushed him forward, he was looking straight at the windscreen of the Duke's Mercedes. That was when he saw it. Duke Seuchar had a 'Board Member' VIP parking permit for Easter Road.

"I want to talk to my lawyer," said Mr Bunnet, "as soon as we get to Edinburgh."

The agent laughed.

"Our orders are to take you straight to Skye. There'll be no need for lawyers. They've got their own ways on the islands."

— ♦ —

Kitty was playing football with Ross Murray, on the small area of grass at the side of the manse, when her phone buzzed. It was a text from her dad.

"Sat 9 Aug 1952."

"What's that?" asked Ross, looking over her shoulder.

"It's an old Hearts game," explained Kitty. "Hearts vs Rangers at Tynecastle, Hearts won 5-0."

"How on earth do you know the score from a game in 1952?" asked Ross.

Kitty laughed.

"What team do you support?" she asked.

Ross had just passed his SFA linesman course, and the training was fresh in his mind.

"As an SFA official," he said, "I have to be neutral. I don't support any team."

"OK," said Kitty, "but when the SFA gives out free tickets to referees and linesmen, whose tickets do you put in for?"

"Rangers, of course," said Ross, "like everybody else."

"Well," said Kitty, "things are a bit different when you support Hearts. You've got to go back a bit to find a game where Hearts beat

Rangers 5-0. My dad has that game recorded. I can't remember how often I've seen it. Hold on, I'll just text him and ask why he sent it."

She got her phone out and started to message, but her dad's phone was not online. She checked the Find My Friends map, and it didn't have a location. In desperation, she even tried a voice call - it didn't connect.

"That's strange. He's turned his phone off."

She thought for a minute about why her dad might text her that date. Her face turned deathly pale.

"Oh shit," she said, "Five-Oh at home!"

"What's wrong? That's a good score."

"Five-Oh is the polis! My dad was telling me the polis are at our house. Then he turned his phone off."

"If the police are after you, you can't stay here," said Ross. "McCallister won't like it if they come to the manse."

"Where am I supposed to go?" demanded Kitty. "I can't go home. We're getting married in two weeks. You're supposed to help me!"

Ross hadn't thought of this consequence of their engagement, but based on his memories of TV and movies, he recognised it was an accepted social convention. But what to do?

"My mum said if I ever got in trouble with the police, I was to turn my phone off and come straight home. That's what we should do: once we get to the castle, mum and dad will sort it."

Kitty turned off her phone. They got their coats and walked to Waverley Station, where they took the next train to Blair Atholl.

— ♦ —

In the arcade on South Bridge, Mary had leveraged her status as Elizabeth's sister into having the run of the place - except, of course, for the secret planning room. Mary's principal interest was the broken-down mechanical machines in the storage room. She'd brought her toolkit from the shed at home, cleared a space to use as a workshop and had already got two of the old machines working. Air Hockey and Penny Falls. Now it was time to thoroughly test them before moving on. The Air Hockey machine required two players and Claire had volunteered for the task. Claire's reactions were fast, and she was leading 3-1 when Mary's phone buzzed.

"Sat 9 Aug 1952."

Mary figured out the coded warning even faster than Kitty and, as an aspiring novelist, Claire had read sufficient crime fiction to know what to do.

"Are you involved in whatever he was up to? Are they going to be looking for you?"

"Mibby."

"You need to get out of the arcade right now!"

"I've got nowhere to go! James will help me."

"If they are looking for you, they'll be tracking your phone. It'll bring them straight here."

Mary took her phone out.

"I'll turn it off."

"If your phone is off, the first place they're going to look for you is the last spot the network saw it. We need to get it away from here before we turn it off. Give me the phone, I'll go somewhere crowded away from the arcade and then turn it off. You go and talk to James."

Claire grabbed her coat and left the arcade with Mary's phone.

As usual, James was playing TDA on the computer in his office. Mary gave him a shake.

"James, the cops are at my house, and I think my dad is on the run. I've got nowhere to go."

"Why don't you phone your mum or Elizabeth?"

"If the cops are after us, they'll be watching our phones. Claire took my phone away from the arcade."

"That's smart," said James, "But what about your new fiancé, isn't he rich? They're more careful about doing surveillance on rich people with lawyers. Why not ask him to help? You can call him from my PC. I've got an app that'll bounce the packets around enough to make it untraceable."

Mary called Dick Seuchar.

"Hi Dick, it's Mary."

"Who?"

"Mary Bunnet, your fiancé! You traded with McCallister."

"Oh, yeah, hi Mary, sorry, I'm a bit wrecked."

"You've got to help me! My dad's on the run from the cops. I need somewhere to hide."

"What the fuck?"

"I need somewhere to hide from the cops until we are married. Can I stay in your mum and dad's house?"

"Of course not! We can't have the police coming to Rimswell House looking for you."

"I can't go home. I need to go somewhere."

"Hold on, I'll ask my dad what to do."

"He says you can go to my grannies' house, but you need to get there by yourself and you need to lose the cops before going anywhere near the place. We are a respectable family with private business interests, and we do not want police with a warrant to search for you on our premises."

"You're not going to help?"

"I'll call my grannies and say you're coming. But my dad says I've not to get in trouble with the cops again, and anyway I can't swim."

"What do you mean 'again' - and what's swimming got to do with it?"

"They live on Inchkeith Island, in the middle of the Forth."

"Jesus, your family is weirder than mine! Are your grandads on the island, too?"

"My grannies are a couple. It used to be a big family secret, but these days nobody cares. Forty years ago, my father's mother, Lesley-Ann Seuchar, fell in love with Pandropa Minto. Lesley-Ann wanted to go down to Seuchar Country, but the only property the family would let her have was Inchkeith Island."

— ♦ —

"How can I get to Inchkeith Island?" asked Mary.

"If the cops are looking for you it's not just your phone we need to worry about. There's also face recognition on CCTV," said Claire.

"And I don't want them coming after me for helping you," said James.

Claire got Google Maps up on her phone.

"There's the island. It's out in the Forth, about three kilometres north of Leith. You're going to need a boat to get there, but if you pay somebody to take you, it will create a trail the cops could follow."

"I had a couple of lessons in a kayak at school," said Mary, "and a couple of times on the canal from one of the rental places."

"I had a go when I was doing my PhD," said James. "They made our group go to the University's place on Loch Tay for team building one year. I was useless, and I hated it. But, I'm fitter now, maybe I'd be OK."

Kayaking and canoeing had become popular activities over the last twenty years as the city had constructed new canals and artificial lakes to adapt to climate change. Edinburgh was warmer and there was now a distinct rainy season in the Autumn. There was also a new seawall along the Forth to deal with the half-metre rise in sea level. The wall had been constructed a hundred metres out into the estuary to create new land for development, and the reclaimed land required a network of drainage canals.

"You could walk down to Princes Street Gardens," said Claire. "There's a big boat rental place on Nor'Loch under the castle. They've got kayaks and they'll rent you one for a few days. Just say you're going up the canal towards Glasgow and doing a couple of nights camping. But actually head out to Portobello and through the sea-lock."

"And then we take a rental kayak out on the Forth at night? We'll die!" said Mary.

"If you get a decent tandem kayak, a proper sea kayak, and you get some practice in the canal before you put it in the sea, and you are lucky with the tide, maybe you'll be lucky. You're both young and fit. The weather is good, and it isn't that far. It's midsummer, and it won't get dark until really late."

James was looking at the map.

"Why don't we get the tram to Leith and rent a kayak there? It's closer to the island. According to Google, there's a place on the drainage canal just behind the seawall."

"Yeah, it's a shorter distance in the kayak, but there's CCTV on the trams. You can walk to Princes Street Gardens and as soon as you are on the canal, there's no cameras. Don't take too long thinking about it. If the cops are tracking Mary's phone, they'll have seen it was in the arcade for a few hours this afternoon. They may turn up and ask questions."

"OK," said James, "that decides it. There's no time. Mary, get your coat. We're going to rent a kayak."

It was only a short walk from the arcade, along South Bridge to the Royal Mile and then down the Mound to Princes Street Gardens.

The attendant in the boat rental place in the gardens was happy enough to rent them a two person rigid sea kayak and wetsuits for two days. James was fairly sure he realised they didn't have a clue what they were doing. His main concern was to ensure they understood that if they brought the boat back early, they'd still be charged for the full two days. Probably he was used to customers with over ambitious plans and just assumed that they'd not get far enough to be in any danger.

The tandem kayak was large and heavy. The staff got it off the rack and into the water for them. They put on the wet suits and stowed their things in a watertight compartment in the middle of the boat. The attendant held the boat against the jetty while they got in, handed them the paddles, and pushed it off into the Nor'loch. Mary was in the front seat and James was in the back. She started to paddle. James tried to copy her movements, but their paddles kept hitting against each other.

"Stop paddling!" said Mary. "You're just getting in the way. Let me do it on my own."

James was frustrated. He had paid for the boat and he wanted a go.

"We both need to paddle. It's a two seat boat!"

"Yeah, but not right now. First, we have to get away from the dock so the guy doesn't see how useless we are and calls us back in. We told him we were experienced. They shouldn't rent a boat like this to beginners, because you need to know how to get out if it rolls over so you don't drown. Beginners get an open boat."

"Hold on, I don't know how to deal with a roll!" said James.

"Too late," said Mary, "just stop paddling until I get us somewhere quieter, then we can practice."

The boat moved slowly with only Mary paddling, but it moved in the direction she intended and they were quickly away from the boat rental shop, across the Nor'loch and turning left on the Union Canal extension towards Portobello.

"OK, it's your turn to paddle," said Mary. "Straight down the canal. You have to use your core muscles. I'll keep my paddle out of your way."

"What core muscles?" asked James. "I'm a gamer, not an athlete."

"Well, if you don't have any now, you will have by tomorrow," laughed Mary. "We've got maybe three kilometres to Portobello, then we need to get the boat to the sea, then maybe 4 or 5km to Inchkeith Island and I have no idea about tides."

"Great!" said James. "I'll give it a try. But if we've not got paddling this thing worked out by Portobello, or it's a lot harder than we thought in the sea, we chuck it in."

"Agreed," said Mary. "I'd rather get caught by the cops than drown."

After about fifteen minutes, James could paddle well enough to keep the boat moving and avoid hitting other canal users and the sides of the canal. They'd gone through the tunnel at the station and were now approaching Holyrood Park.

"I'm getting tired," said James.

"OK, I'll take over until after the Palace," said Mary, "then we need to practice both paddling together. I'm in the front, so my job is to keep an even stroke and your job is to follow it and not bash your paddle against mine."

Eventually they managed to get a rhythm, and the boat was moving easily and quickly. Soon they arrived at the lock which separated the canal from the sea. On their right, just before the lock, was a ramp for taking boats in and out of the water.

"What do you think?" said James.

"It's only 8 o'clock. We've got another few hours of light. We can do it."

"OK, let's go for it!"

They paddled across to the ramp. Mary got out before the boat completely grounded and grabbed the front. They lifted the boat between them and padded up the ramp and past the lock. There was no ramp on the other side of the lock, but it was easy enough to walk across the beach to the sea and launch the boat again.

The sea felt very different from the smooth water of the canal. Luckily, it was a pleasant summer evening, and there wasn't much swell. They could see Inchkeith island slightly upriver and nearer the other side of the Firth. The tide was against them, but there were two of them paddling; the boat had no problem with the conditions and they could make some headway. They should have had something to eat and a rest before starting off, but youth and luck compensated for inexperience. The vast bulk of Arseny Parslikov's yacht the Admiral

Pemberlov stood out in the Firth even more clearly visible than the island. It took a couple of hours, but they made it to Inchkeith just as it was getting dark enough for the automatic lighthouse to turn on its beam. As they circled, looking for a beach to land the kayak, they got a closeup view of the yacht moored only a hundred metres away. Each of the three hulls was secured by two massive anchor chains and a thick electric cable stretched from the central hull to a newly constructed concrete substation building on the island. Their circumnavigation of the island took them right underneath the cable. Finally, they found a suitable spot. They beached the kayak, got out and carried it a safe distance from the water.

Dick's grannies had been keeping an eye out for their arrival and came over the grass to meet them. The grannies lived in an old fort on the island. It was a large building, only a small part of which had been renovated for habitation, but the views from their dining room, which had once been a gun emplacement, out over the Firth towards the bridges were extraordinary. Conveniently, the island was home to wild chickens and sheep: dinner was roast chicken and potatoes from the grannies' garden.

Their hosts could see that James and Mary were exhausted from their journey, so as soon as dinner was finished, they suggested they might want to turn in. To protect their grandson's interests, they thoughtfully provided separate bedrooms.

— ♦ —

"Would you like to come with us to visit the Admiral Pemberlov?" asked Granny Seuchar-Minto at breakfast the next day. "Mr Parslikov is away and his housekeeper offered to give us a tour of the house and gardens today. I'm sure she wouldn't mind if you came along too."

James and Mary readily agreed and so they joined the grannies in their motorboat for the short journey to the superyacht. They were warmly greeted by Arseny's housekeeper at the boat dock at the rear of the central hull. They took the lift up from the dock and emerged in a circular hallway. A spiral staircase continued upwards and there was a heavy wooden door in front of them. The housekeeper placed her finger on a scanner to open the door and beckoned them out onto the deck.

"Welcome to the Admiral Pemberlov," she said.

The yacht had been impressive from a distance, but it was something else again up close. Behind them, the circular building they had emerged from proved to be a stone folly in the same style as the main house. Facing them across a formal garden with neatly trimmed hedges, fountains and a decorative lake was a magnificent country house. Directly above the central courtyard of the house, the control tower of an aircraft carrier rose fifty metres into the air, topped with a radar antenna. The housekeeper led them up the gravel drive towards the house while reciting information about the yacht.

"The Admiral Pemberlov was constructed in 2045 in St. Petersburg, Russia. It is a trimaran construction. Each of the hulls was formerly an aircraft carrier. Arsey…" she paused, "I'm sorry, I was his nanny and I'm used to the family's pet name from when he was small. Mr Parslikov acquired the aircraft carriers as military surplus and commissioned the yard to repurpose them as a superyacht. The control towers of two of the carriers were discarded, and the control tower of the third carrier was mounted directly above the house. A framework of steel tubes connects the carrier hulls together to form a rigid structure, and a 500 metre by 500 metre steel deck was constructed over the trimaran hulls. The new deck overlaps the hulls by approximately fifty metres on each side. The entire deck was covered in two metres of rocks and soil to provide a suitable surface for cultivation."

"And what about the house?" asked James.

"Mr Arsey commissioned an exact 3D scan of the original courtyard of Chatworth house in England. Each individual stone was cut by robotic equipment to be the duplicate of one in Chatworth and the house was then reconstructed above the central hull of Admiral Pemberlov. The house is sixty metres long by fifty metres wide and three stories high. A steel frame hidden within the walls on the courtyard side of the house provides support for the control tower of the third aircraft carrier. The captain and crew live in the central carrier's crew accommodation and work in the control tower. The house itself is purely for Mr Arsey, his servants and guests."

The view was certainly extraordinary. The contrast between the yellow-brown stone of the seventeenth century country house and the grey steel and antennas of the aircraft carrier control tower directly above it was particularly striking.

"Would you like to take the path through the orchard and visit the stables and conservatory or should we go directly up the drive to the house?" asked the housekeeper as they came to a fork in the path.

A debate broke out as the Grannies wanted to see the house, but Mary wanted to see the horses. It was interrupted by the sound of a helicopter approaching from the north. The housekeeper turned in the direction of the noise and shaded her eyes with her hand.

"Excuse me, that is Mr Arsey returning. I must go to meet him. Can I ask you to explore the grounds on your own for a few minutes? I will return as soon as possible."

A self-driving golf-buggy came quickly towards them along the drive, presumably summoned by the housekeeper. She walked towards it; it stopped as soon as it got close to her. She got in and it drove away, heading for the opposite side of the house. The helicopter was also converging on a landing spot on that side of the house.

"Well, well," said the first Granny, "I was told Mr Parslikov was in Taymouth Castle for a few days. I wasn't expecting to meet him."

James wasn't sure he wanted to meet Arseny Parslikov. He wouldn't have come if he'd known Arseny would be there. But it was too late now and there was no doubt the yacht was impressive.

They walked over to the ornamental pond in front of the house so the Grannies could sit down for a few minutes and Mary could take selfies. After a few minutes, the golf buggy returned and James was surprised to see Arseny had come to meet them himself.

"I have brought towels, I am going for a swim," said Arseny. "Would you like to join me? Or perhaps you would prefer a tour of the house. There is a lot of old furniture and paintings and shit."

The Grannies decided to take up the offer of a tour of the house with the housekeeper. Mary put her hand in the water to check the temperature.

"It's warm!" she said.

"Of course," said Arseny, "there is no shortage of hot water on my boat."

He took his robe off and jumped into the pond. It was more like a small lake than a large pool. Mary stared at his abs and the bulge in his far-too-tight speedos.

Arseny noticed and laughed.

"Elizabeth says you like billionaire romance novels," he said, "so what do you think? Would I make the cover?"

Mary nodded.

"James," said Arseny, "I have something to discuss with you. Please join me. There are extra towels and robes on the buggy."

Ever since he'd sold his excess fat to the butcher in the city farm, James was less embarrassed about his body. He stripped to his underpants and jumped into the pool. The warm water felt great. He'd not been swimming for years. He did a couple of lengths and then swam over to Arseny. He was pretty sure he knew what this was about.

"Is this about Elizabeth?" he asked. "Are you interested in trading?"

Arseny smiled.

"Are you interested in marrying Elizabeth?" he asked.

"I like her," said James, "but I think she's looking for someone richer than me who wants to have a child. She said she would prefer to be traded."

"I thought so," said Arseny, "but what about you? Do you want to be married? Do you even like girls?"

"I'd like to be married some time," said James, "but I'm not sure just yet. And I do like girls. I'd probably marry Elizabeth if she was interested, but I don't think I'm rich enough for her. And I'm not sure I'm ready to look after a child."

Arseny looked at him.

"I bet you've got a female identity," he said. "I have had many lovers. Women and men. I can tell these things."

"Yeah, so what? Everybody has both identities these days."

"Elizabeth, interests me," said Arseny. "I could go to England and have my pick of women who could bear children. But marrying Elizabeth would allow me to claim Scottish citizenship and our child would also be a citizen. That could be useful if I ever fall out with the government in Russia. An occupational hazard for oligarchs, you understand: that and falling out of windows."

"So, do you want to make me an offer?" asked James.

"Perhaps, I am not sure. What should I offer?"

"Elizabeth was first in the draft. If you want to trade for her, you'll either need to offer more than one pick or a pick plus money."

Arseny laughed. "A negotiator. I like that. But, you know I did not make a choice in the draft, I do not have a pick of my own to trade. So just money. How much do you want?"

"One million euro," said James. "There are only five girls in Scotland who can have children and many rich men who want to have an heir."

Arseny laughed and slapped James on the shoulder.

"Well played!" he said. "But I think not. There are two problems with your offer."

"What's that?" asked James. He felt things were going downhill fast. He really didn't want to end up with nothing and look like an idiot in front of Alexandra.

"First," said Arseny, "there is the Jus Primae Noctis problem. She only has a licence for one baby and the King is going to get first crack at her. From what I am told, the chances of her baby being the king's child are high. There's no premium on the basis of Elizabeth producing an heir unless you can solve that problem."

"OK," said James, "and what is the second problem?"

"The second problem is if I ask her, she'll probably say yes, even if I don't make a deal with you. Why wouldn't she?"

"If she gets engaged or marries anyone else before a year is up without being traded, then she'll be banned from future drafts."

"And why would that worry her if she was married to a billionaire?"

"She'd be taking a risk. If she got engaged to you and you didn't end up getting married, she'd find it difficult to find someone else."

"We could just walk straight into church and get married without getting engaged first. Nobody would know until it was a done deal. So no risk."

James could feel his opportunity slipping through his fingers.

"I guess you're not going to make me an offer then?"

"I like you, James, so I'll just tell you how it is going to be. In a few days, there will be a wedding at Taymouth Castle. The Murrays and the Mintos are going to preempt the Jus Primae Noctis thing by not telling the King about their marriages until after they are over. I'll be marrying Elizabeth. I hope there are no hard feelings. It is just business, but I'm not going to pay for your option."

"Maybe a million is too much, but you could offer something. What would a few hundred thousand euro matter to you? This yacht must be worth a billion."

"You have much to learn about business, James. You think this yacht cost me a billion euro? Guess again."

"At least 500 million. It's the biggest yacht in the world by far."

"Try fifty million."

"No way!"

"The Russian government gave me the yacht for free and pays me fifty million a year."

"You're kidding! Who did you have to bribe to get that deal?"

"Nobody. It is a good deal for them. The only condition is that I must not sail her within 1,000 kilometres of Moscow for the next fifty years."

"Oh, shit." said James. "That's why the pool is so warm, isn't it?"

"Don't worry," said Arseny, "there's a heat exchanger, it isn't the actual cooling water. The water in the swimming pool is only slightly radioactive. I love swimming in my pool at night. When it's really dark, you can just make out the beautiful blue glow."

"So these three aircraft carriers still have their reactors. The fuel isn't removed?"

"Actually, the Russian aircraft carriers had diesel engines. It's the reactors from decommissioned Northern Fleet nuclear submarines that are stored below us on the deck where they used to keep the planes. It'd cost them a lot more than giving me a yacht to decommission twenty submarine reactors at their present level of radioactivity. After fifty years, the radiation will have fallen enough that the work is affordable."

"So you are being paid to keep their radioactive waste away from Moscow until it has decayed enough to be safe. That's disgusting."

"You are from Edinburgh. Why are you so surprised by this deal? Didn't you Scots get paid by England to store their old nuclear submarines in Rosyth, four hundred miles away from London, for fifty years because they didn't want to pay for the decommissioning?"

"Actually, they didn't pay us," said James. "They just left them in Rosyth and nobody said anything."

Arseny laughed and laughed to the point he almost choked.

— ♦ —

James and Mary decided to risk the radiation and soak in Arseny's hot tub until the grannies were finished with their tour of the house. Their abs and biceps were aching after the unaccustomed exercise of the previous day, the warm water was soothing and Arseny was good company.

When the grannies returned, they were not accompanied by the housekeeper but a tall young woman with long blond hair which fell over her shoulders. She was wearing a jet-black military uniform with polished knee-length boots and a sidearm holster. A box cutter protruded from the breast pocket of her dress uniform tunic. There were three patches on the arm. The first was a lightning bolt, the second was a set of blue wavy lines and the third depicted a pair of long-nosed pliers.

"Allow me to introduce my sister," said Arseny. "Senior Lieutenant Georgiana Parslikovna of the KGB."

James eyes naturally fell on the new arrivals chest and he was disconcerted to see a drop of red fluid on the small section of blade protruding from the top of the box cutter.

Georgiana greeted James and Mary with a firm handshake.

"My friends call me Peggy," she smiled, "are any of your sisters out, Miss Bunnet?"

"I'm afraid not," replied Mary, "although mother did provide us all with male names in case we should like to go that way. Mine is Fred."

"Ah," said Georgiana with a smile, "you are the third sister: your mother was obviously inspired by the classics."

"Georgiana called in some favours from the Second Directorate and we managed to locate Mr Whackov and Lydia," said Arseny. "I'm sure she will be able to persuade Whackov to do the right thing."

"Give me one more day," said Georgiana. "His nuts are proving tougher to crack than I expected."

Arseny grabbed the side of the pool and, flexing his sizeable biceps, pushed himself up and out of the water. He picked up a towel.

"I think I shall return to Taymouth Castle now. It is time for me to make my proposal to Elizabeth. Mary, you can fly with me if you like. Your fiancé, Mr Seuchar, is also travelling to the castle and Lydia is already there."

"We'll be going now too," said Granny Seuchar-Minto. "It was a pleasure to meet you James."

"Hold on," said James. "I need a ride back to Edinburgh."

"Ah," said Arseny, "I'm afraid not. It will be more convenient if you stay here as my guest for a few days. I shall return with Elizabeth after we are married, and you may join us on our honeymoon."

Arseny turned and walked towards his helicopter. Mary got out of the pool and followed him.

"Why don't you put on some clothes?" suggested Georgiana and rested her right hand on the handle of her service automatic.

Behind them, James heard the helicopter rotors spinning up and then saw it take off and head off towards the north. He was getting nervous.

"I think I'd prefer to leave," said James.

"Of course," said Georgiana, "let me show you the way off the ship."

They walked across the lawn, crossing a small grove of trees until they came to a waist-high privet hedge. At one point, a gap had been left in the hedge and a diving board installed.

"The hedge is the only barrier at the edge of the deck, so you want to be careful. We installed the diving board because it's a Russian Navy tradition that sailors newly posted to an aircraft carrier should jump off the flight deck into the water."

"You make the crew walk the plank?"

"Actually, there are surprisingly few injuries."

"Right," said James.

"Anyway," said Georgiana, "it's about thirty metres down to the river and then about a hundred metres swim to the island and a few kilometres kayaking to the shore. You are welcome to leave any time you like. Or you can enjoy our hospitality until Arseny and Elizabeth return. What I would not recommend is trying to get into the lower decks to reduce the distance to the water. The radiation down there is far more dangerous than the dive."

"Thanks for the advice," said James. He walked over to the edge and looked down. It was a hell of a long way.

"Come on then," said Georgiana, "come to the house. I'll show you around."

They walked across the lawns to reach the gravel drive, which brought them to the formal front entrance of the house. Georgiana led James up a grandiose marble staircase. Portraits of the Parslikov ancestors decorated the walls.

"I have to get back to work in a minute, so I'll just show you where you'll be sleeping: feel free to wander around. Please don't try to get into the control tower or any of the ship's systems. The crew are armed and usually drunk. They can be trigger-happy."

They reached the third floor and turned left on a wide corridor which led around the central courtyard.

"This is my brother's bedroom," said Georgiana. "Mine is next door. You can sleep here until he returns with Elizabeth."

The centrepiece of the room was a magnificent fourposter bed. The windows opened onto a small balcony with a view over the Pemberlov estate to the Forth and the coast of Fife. But James's attention was drawn to the bed.

"Yes," said Georgiana, with a chuckle, "each one of the vertical notches on the headboard is one of my brother's conquests. Where he's drawn a straight line across the notch it's a female, where there's a little arrow it is a male and where there are two vertical lines close together, it was twins."

"I see," said James.

"But the best bit is over here," said Georgiana, and opened a polished wooden door to the left of the bed.

"This is my brother's sex dungeon," she said. "Don't look so surprised. All billionaires with helicopters, yachts and six-pack abs have sex dungeons these days!"

James was impressed. He had never seen so many whips, canes, chains, and dildos before in his life. And, the previous year, in his female identity Miranda, he'd been hired as an escort for a council function at Edinburgh City Chambers.

"I'll leave you to it," she said. "I have to get back to Mr Whackov now. I hope the screaming doesn't keep you awake."

— ♦ —

Georgiana's bedroom was next to Arseny's, but instead of a sex dungeon, she had an en-suite torture chamber. Unfortunately, the walls were not as soundproof as might be expected in an old country house.

"And now I shall don the instrument," James heard Georgiana say, "and you know what follows."

James heard the sound of buckles being tightened, followed by the creak of a bedspring. Then Mr Whackov screamed. The noises continued and James left Arseny's bedroom in search of somewhere quieter and less distracting. There was a well-stocked drinks cabinet in one of the reception rooms downstairs, and James retrieved a bottle of vodka and collected one of the robes from the pool. He walked over to the point on the deck where the hedge was broken and the diving board stuck out over the edge of the ship. Georgiana had said that it was fairly safe. He went up to the edge and peeked over. It was a hell of a long way down. He opened the vodka and took a good gulp. It was still a hell of a long way down. He put on the robe for a little extra warmth and sat on the diving board. After two more gulps, it still looked like a long way. He tried to build himself up to running along the board and off into space. It wasn't happening.

Gradually, James's attempt at finding courage in the vodka bottle, combined with tiredness after the previous days' exertions and the excitement of today, turned into sleepiness. It was a sunny late afternoon. He pulled up the hood on the robe and lay down on the grass near the diving board. Soon he was asleep. When he woke up, it was already dark, probably getting on for midnight. It was warm enough; the alcohol hadn't completely worn off and he couldn't be bothered walking all the way back to the house. He wondered if KGB torturers clocked off at five o'clock or kept it up all night. If Peggy Parslikovna was still at it, there was no way he could sleep in Arseny's room. He drank a couple more gulps of vodka, found two more robes beside the pool to use as a blanket and a pillow, and settled down again on the grass.

When he woke again, there was a glimmer of light in the sky. Somebody was shaking his shoulder. He opened one eye. The person leaning over him was wearing a wetsuit. There was fur on their face and they had whiskers.

"Miaow!" said the cat person.

James looked at his vodka bottle. Then he remembered.

"Justine?"

"Shh!" said Justine, "I've come to rescue you. Unless you want to be here, in which case I'll leave you to it. We weren't sure."

"No, I'd quite like to be rescued, thanks. I don't have the nerve to jump in the water and swim, and that's the only way off this yacht."

"Cats don't like swimming either," she said, "so I brought a boat and a rope and a climbing harness. Do you know how to abseil?"

"I've done it in games," said James, "but not in real life."

"Please forget whatever you did in videogames. Most likely it will get you killed. I'll set it up so I can lower you and you don't have to do anything."

"Great!"

Justine showed him how to adjust the harness. She tied a figure-of-eight knot on a bite of rope, hooked it onto a carabiner, and clipped it to his belay loop. She used the steel rail on the side of the diving board as an anchor and threaded the rope through her belay device.

"Don't touch the carabiner until you are in the boat. Once you are safe, unclip it."

"OK."

Justine took in the slack and got ready.

"You're all set. Claire and Victoria will bring the boat underneath you."

James hesitated.

"I've got you," said Justine. "This rope could hold a small car, but you've got to go over the side before I can start lowering you. Face in, take it easy, and push off the side of the ship with your legs if you swing in."

There was nothing for it. James carefully sat down on the edge of the ship and let himself go. He fell a few feet, then the rope came tight and stretched and he came to a stop a few metres below the deck with a gentle bounce. Justine started to lower him. He looked down and saw a jet-black inflatable rib. Claire and Victoria were using paddles to keep it in place underneath him. Justine lowered him slowly. She couldn't see what was happening from her position and she wanted to make it easy for Claire and Victoria to bring him into the boat. She felt the rope go slack when James reached the boat and unclipped. She pulled it back up, removed her harness, loaded the rope and climbing gear into her rucksack, and tossed it down to the boat.

Despite the protests of her cat side, the human part of Justine had decided that a diving board was too much of an opportunity to ignore. She adjusted the tension of the board, took a couple of trial bounces and then went for it. Ten years ago, when she was at University she'd learned how to somersault off the three-metre springboard at the Commonwealth Pool and had tried the ten-metre board a few times. The principle was the same; it was just much further to the water.

She hit the water harder than she expected, but the wetsuit helped absorb the impact and she was soon back in the boat. They paddled silently away from the Admiral Pemberlov towards Inchkeith island where they retrieved the rented kayak. Justine powered up the outboard motor, and they turned towards Edinburgh, towing the kayak behind them.

No longer marooned, James looked out across the Forth and saw there was sunshine on Leith.

15:10 to Waverley

Madame Margaret Noyce still lived in the double upper flat in Springvalley Gardens she had once shared with her husbands. At work, she had been known by her maiden name Margaret Noyce and following Chief Constable Merilees' death, she'd switched from Noyce-Merilees to straightforward Noyce in her private life as well. For the last few years, like most of the senior Guild members, she'd acquired an Alexandra to manage her business interests day-to-day. The company she'd founded with Professor Hume and Dr Knox to purchase the Edinburgh Brothel all those years ago had grown large enough to acquire the McLeod corporation assets in the US when Mr McLeod was declared dead. Now, their US operation was in negotiation with the US Department of Justice to take over the entire Federal Penitentiary system and run it as a profit-generating business using the technology and processes pioneered in Scotland. It was a tremendous opportunity and one which was naturally being resisted fiercely by the incumbent prison management companies. With the contract requiring approval from Congressional committees and scepticism from Republican lawmakers about closing conventional prisons, everything had to run smoothly in Scotland. Up to now, a few inmates fleeing into the forest had been a minor problem, but with the US deal in the balance, any suggestion that the tracking bracelets were ineffective or could be circumvented was a threat to a trillion-dollar opportunity.

If you were to walk down Springvalley Gardens and glance at Madame Noyce's building, you would see no reason for a wealthy person to choose to live there. It was just another pleasant street in Morningside. The reason for Madame Noyce's choice - or more accurately, the choice of her deceased husbands - was only visible when you looked out the rear windows of her flat. Even after all these years, the view from her bedroom window brought a smile to her face every time she woke. Right in the middle of Edinburgh, hidden from the street by the surrounding tenements, was a miniature Wild-West town. It had started out as a false front on a furniture warehouse. The warehouse was long out of business, but over time, a series of proprietors had adopted the western town and considerably embellished it. There was a saloon and a sheriff's office, an undertaker and a general store. Her second husband had been a huge fan of cowboy movies and as soon as they viewed the flat, his mind was made up. The place had grown on her and, after her husbands died, she had bought the Western town for the McLeod Corporation.

One of the buildings she had acquired was the former Morningside library. The front of the library was on the busy Morningside Road, but the rear opened onto the Wild West Town street and had an appropriate facade. Her original plan had been to use the premises as a Wild West themed saloon and brothel, but that had been a step too far for the douce citizens of Morningside and the council had put a stop to the idea. Instead, the old library was now used as corporate offices for the McLeod Corporation. Further down the street, a building which looked like a livery stable was a false front on garage space. The Western Town had always been more of a personal project for Madame Noyce. Much of the space was unused, but recently it had acquired a new tenant. The sheriff's office was now the official registered office of Claverhouse and Company. The logic of a sheriff's officer firm operating out of the sheriff's office was so profound neither Justine nor Madame Noyce had raised an objection when the Alexandras suggested it. The only noticeable changes as a result of the new tenant were that Justine's old cat basket - constructed from a crate which had once held assault rifles and an EU special forces issue sleeping bag - now sat in a quiet and warm corner of the office and the 'Sheriff' sign above the door had 'Claverhouse and Company' inserted above it and the word 'Officer' under it. The font on the new text was small enough that you needed to be really close up before you noticed the additions. The vehicles which Justine had acquired in the auction at the Royal Highland Show had been patched up sufficiently to get an MOT and were now parked in the garage behind the 'livery stable'.

Madame Noyce poured her coffee into a camping mug, picked up her morning bottle of Brothel Fuel and, as every morning, took the short walk from her flat to the sheriff's office to have breakfast with a hologram of her dead second husband. Both her husbands' consciousness had been uploaded to the cloud by the Guild and they now lived in the virtual world of video games. The jail in the Western town had been remodelled to exactly match the Sheriff's office in Amarillo in Red Lead Redaction, the Guild's computers could project his image as a hologram in the sheriff's office and insert her avatar into the matching space in his virtual world. There were other ways of being together, but this was her favourite. If she had time, she might even dress in western clothes to perfect the illusion, but today the only nod to the Western setting was her jeans and white shirt.

"Howdy, Margaret," said the Sheriff, "Your Alexandra was looking for you. I told her you weren't here yet, and she started one of the bounty missions. She'll be back in a few minutes."

"That girl never stops," observed Madame Noyce.

"Yeah," replied the Sheriff, "She's a grinder. She's got no interest in fighting other players or just chilling and riding about. She must have far more money and gold than she could possibly need, but she's always running missions and collecting stuff to get more. I think she's trying to buy every single thing in the game."

"And what's she going to do, then?" asked Madame Noyce.

"I guess she'll get bored and switch to TDA 6," said the Sheriff, "she's not really cut out for Red Lead Redaction, she can't just relax and appreciate the scenery or a long horse ride."

At that moment, the door of the sheriff's office flew open, and a body was thrown on the floor beside his desk.

"Maude Nicolls," said Alexandra.

The Sheriff yawned and opened his desk drawer. He pulled out a wad of bills and counted off two.

"She's worth more alive, Alexandra," he said.

"I know, but I worked it out, and it's more efficient this way. I make less money per bounty, but I finish faster and don't lose as many."

As she was talking, the body on the floor despawned, leaving only a patch of blood.

"Hello Alexandra," said Madame Noyce, "what's new this morning?"

The Sheriff went to his stove and brought back a tin cup full of coffee for Alexandra.

"Not much," said Alexandra. "The American deal is still buried in the appropriations committee. We'll get it in the end, but the competition has friends in Congress and is going to fight us at every step. The only other thing is the Madame of the brothel in Pitlochry called."

"I didn't even know we had a brothel in Pitlochry!" said Madame Noyce.

"Yes, we opened a small community brothel in the back of the police station a couple of years ago. It's been doing quite well."

"What did she want?"

"She wants us to send her more staff. Apparently, the hotels are full of rich Tories and tradespeople. She said the local minister usually has a blow job, but he booked a VIP suite and three girls this week and told them he'd just collected a big fee for a wedding at Taymouth Castle."

Madame Noyce put down her coffee. A frown crossed her brow.

"Alexandra, check the location of the Bunnet sisters. The ones the King asserted Jus Primae Noctis on."

"Elizabeth Bunnet, Jane Bunnet, Mary Bunnet, Kitty Bunnet and Lydia Bunnet are all in Taymouth Castle. So is Mrs Bunnet."

"Shit!" observed Madame Noyce. "I spent a lot of money on the TV rights to their defloration and it looks like they have skipped town. They are supposed to ask permission before leaving the City of Edinburgh."

"Are those the sisters that have the licence from Italy to have a child?" asked the Sheriff.

"Yes, that's them. And I will bet they are skipping town because their husbands don't want the King impregnating them before they get the chance to do it themselves," said the Madame. "Alexandra…"

"I know," said Alexandra, "put out a bounty on the Bunnets. Dead or alive. I'll get started on the poster."

"Definitely not dead," said the Madame, "Half a million euro to bring back all five Bunnet sisters, in good health and before they are married. They're worth more as a set, you know."

"That's a lot of money, even for a prestigious bounty," observed Alexandra.

"It is," said the Madame, "but we have to make an example of them. With the American deal in the balance, the only story about runaways we can afford to have in the press is one about them getting caught."

The poster took shape on the electronic-ink notice board outside the sheriff's office in the Western town and simultaneously on the board outside the Amarillo sheriff's office in the video game. A second later, a copy was messaged to Justine's phone.

There was no way Justine could turn down such a lucrative engagement, but with five targets to capture and almost no time to do it before they were married, she was going to need help.

— ♦ —

The next day, Justine and Victoria went to the arcade immediately after dropping the kids off at school. The newly renovated horse transporter and mobile police station were parked outside. They'd been painted jet black with a gloss finish. The old police lights had been replaced with brand new super-bright LED versions and the sirens with a fully controllable sound synthesiser. There were new official signs reading 'PIMPS', 'POLICE', and 'Mobile Brothel' and in small letters near the bottom of the trailer 'Operated by Claverhouse and Company on behalf of H.M. Brothel.' PIMPS was an acronym for 'Prostitution Inmate Management Police Scotland'. Justine felt like she had grown up all at once: she had an actual company, with an office and lorries and horses. The only fly in the ointment was that some wit had already managed to scrawl the letter 'W' before the word 'HORSES' on her second truck.

Claire and James came out of the arcade carrying coffee and cakes from the arcade cafe. Justine opened the door, and they all climbed into the trailer of the larger lorry. Inside, it was laid out like a miniature police station. There was an office with a table and phone, a break room with a coffee machine and fridge, and the area which had once been a cell had been converted into a small bedroom with a red light to indicate when it was in use. Right at the back of the long vehicle, there was storage space with lockers for equipment.

The door opened again, and the drivers of the two lorries joined them. One looked to be about forty, the other was in his fifties. They were dressed head to toe like extras from a Western movie. Not like cowboys, more like well-to-do townspeople. One had a polished leather gun belt with silver insets.

"We're all loaded up and ready to go, Justine, " said the older man. Then he turned to the others.

"Chief Constable Merilees, Police Scotland, deceased, at your service. Latterly Deputy Chief of Police in Los Espíritus, with responsibility for Robbery Homicide."

The other man tipped his hat.

"Detective Inspector Duncan Chisholm, Police Scotland, deceased. Currently Sheriff of Amarillo. Howdy James, I remember you from the cabin."

"They were my bosses at Police Scotland before the Guild had them killed and uploaded," said Justine. "When they were alive, they were married to Madame Noyce. She asked them to help us."

"Wouldn't miss it. Ain't nothing like a bounty hunting posse!" drawled the Detective Inspector. After living in Red Lead Redaction for almost five years, he'd picked up the accent from NPCs.

"The Chief and the Sheriff are going to drive the trucks," said Justine, "the telepresence robots they've been downloaded into have got code to drive vehicles and they can charge themselves up from the socket in the cab. We will be in the mobile police station."

"What's with the Wild West theme?" asked Victoria.

"It's the Madame's idea," said Justine, "because we'll be using horses. She thinks she'll get more TV coverage of the prisoners getting brought in if we play up the bounty hunter angle. The publicity is an important part of this for the brothel and they are paying top dollar."

Justine pointed at the bounty poster on the e-ink notice board in the conference room.

"Five hundred thousand euro, for the five Bunnet sisters provided we bring them in alive and well and before they are married. They are getting married tomorrow morning in Taymouth Castle."

"How much do we get?" asked Claire.

"Fifty thousand euro each for you, Victoria and James, assuming we do the job properly and the Brothel pays the full 500k," said Justine. "Alexandra worked it out for me. She says I should get the biggest share because I've got an office and trucks and horses and telepresence robots to pay for and also the fuel and ammo."

"That's fair," said James, "and you're the best fighter, anyway."

Claire was slightly concerned that Justine believed that expenditure on ammunition might be a significant cost factor, but she said nothing; 50k was good money.

"Right," said Justine, "raise your right hands and repeat after me."

Victoria laughed.

Claire frowned. She took a different view of things being American. "Come on, this is serious. We've got to be sworn-in to Justine's posse."

"I do solemnly swear…" Justine waited for them to repeat it.

"that I will faithfully execute all lawful precepts…"

"directed to the office of Deputy Sheriff's Officer of the City of Edinburgh…"

"under the authority of Claverhouse and Company…"

"and as a PIMP subcontractor enforce the regulations and discipline of His Majesty's Brothel without malice or favour, returning fugitive employees to lawful custody…"

"and taking only my lawful fees."

"Miaow!" Justine handed each of them a shiny metal Deputy Sheriff Officer badge.

"Just one more thing. It doesn't matter what your personal feelings are about the Bunnet sisters, they are fugitives and you are deputies. I expect everyone in my posse to stay professional. Let's hit the road!"

— ♦ —

It was soon clear that although they'd been fixed up enough to pass their MOTs, the old lorries were not in great condition. The engine in the cab which pulled the mobile police station was making disconcerting noises and running hot. Justine decided they had to push on. If they didn't stay on schedule, they'd lose out on the full 500k payment. The noises from the engine got worse, and it began to steam, but it held out until they turned off into a forestry car park on the hill above Killin.

Justine spread an ancient paper Ordnance Survey map over the table in the mobile police station. There were no modern computer screens in the old vehicle.

"OK, guys. This is the plan. We are here, on the hill just above Killin at the western end of Loch Tay. The wedding is happening tomorrow morning in Taymouth castle. That's beside Kenmore, at the eastern end of the loch. We can't drive these vehicles through Killin. They'd be spotted in a second and somebody would tell Baron Minto. So we're going the rest of the way off the main road, on horseback. Then we camp overnight close to the castle, get up early in the morning, grab the targets, and get out of town and into the hills again. We ride cross-country to Pitlochry and put the prisoners on the 15:10 to Waverley."

"Sounds easy enough," said Victoria. "There's six of us. We're armed. Two of us are bulletproof immortal robots and one of us is a human-labrador-cat chimaera with special forces training. There are only five women to catch."

"You're forgetting the Ath'hole Highlanders," said the Chief Constable.

"What?"

"The Murrays have a private army called the Ath'hole Highlanders. It's the only legal private army in Scotland. They got permission from Queen Victoria. It's a fair bet they're not going to stand by while we grab the heir to the Athole estate's new bride and cart her off to the Brothel."

"Hold on, how come nobody told us about private armies before we got into this!?" asked Claire.

"Don't worry, there's only a few hundred of them," said Justine, "A thousand tops, if you add on the Minto and Seuchar servants. It's just people who work on the Duke's estate. They don't train that much. Remember, we've got horses and we are using small trails through the forest. Cars can't go in there and nobody on foot is going to keep up with a horse."

The Detective Inspector opened the horse transporter and began to bring the animals out. The first one was a silver mare. Justine whistled, and the horse walked over and waited beside her.

Victoria had seen Justine with a silver horse like that before. "Justine, is that Sandy? What happened to his horn?"

Justine laughed. "Check out underneath. Mandy is a mare, Sandy is a stallion. He's somewhere in the forest, I haven't seen him for months. The cops bought Mandy from the Army. She used to do ceremonial duties and pull the coach for the English queen before Independence."

"Isn't she quite old for a horse? I mean, it's nearly twenty-five years since Independence."

"Yeah, but it's not impossible. They can live that long. And she's still very healthy."

"Strange, they have such similar names: Mandy and Sandy, and they're both pure silver."

"I suppose, but it's just a coincidence."

James was the only one who'd never ridden a horse before, so the Amarillo Sheriff helped with his saddle. Justine opened the weapons locker.

"Right Sheriff, here's yours. A pair of Navy revolvers and a carbine repeater. Chief Constable. A Glock and sniper rifle. That's the nearest thing I could find to Los Espíritus PD weapons. I'll take my Europol Glock 19 and a Guild Laser Rifle. Victoria, you get a Guild laser rifle. Claire, you're not authorised to carry firearms. But since you're American, I'm going to give you a Glock, anyway. Best to keep it concealed. Also, Brothel issue tranquilliser dart guns for Claire and James. Everybody gets a Tazer. Victoria, you've got your carbon nanotube cloak and I have my poncho. Claire and James, get a kevlar vest from the locker, just in case. Load up the bivvy gear and food in the saddlebags and let's get moving."

Just before they set off, Justine called Alexandra.

"I've been tracking you," said Alexandra. "I can see you're in the car park in the forest."

"Yeah, we got here, but the cab that pulls the mobile police station doesn't sound good at all, and there's steam coming out. Can you organise to have it fixed? The rest of the plan stays the same."

"I'll try, it might not be easy to find a garage that can handle it because it's so old. Leave it with me."

— ♦ —

They made their way through the forest and skirted round Killin higher up the hillside. Eventually their trail joined the main loch-side road, but by that time it was dark, really dark - the kind of dark you never experience in a city. Justine had excellent night vision and the two telepresence robots could switch to infra-red so they led Victoria, Claire and James's horses. There were a few places where there were buildings close to the road, and they slowed to a crawl to make as little noise as possible. Before they reached the outskirts of Kenmore, they cut off again on a side trail up into the forestry. They crossed open fields and passed an imposing modern farmhouse. Luckily, there was no moon because Mandy's silver coat would have stood out for miles. Finally, they pitched camp in a small plantation above the White Tower of Taymouth Castle. They had camouflage green two-person tents, inflatable camping mattresses, and down sleeping bags. There was Fuel for the humans, and a fuel cell based generator to recharge the robots.

Justine slipped off into the night to hunt something for her supper and returned half an hour later with two rabbits. When she was in the forest, Justine would normally eat the food she caught raw, but to be sociable she skinned and gutted them and cooked them over a small gas camping stove to share with the others.

— ♦ —

They awoke at first light, easy enough to do when you are sleeping in a tent. Breakfast was Brothel Fuel and coffee made on Justine's camping stove. Justine made porridge for herself.

"Why won't you drink Fuel?" asked Claire curiously. "Everybody else does."

"I can smell what's in it, it's not just food. I don't eat stuff that messes with my mind."

"Well, of course, the Brothel Fuel is formulated to enhance employees' libido. That's no secret. But you could drink normal Fuel."

"The normal Fuel has the same additives, just not as much. And they've been increasing the dose. You can't fool a Labrador nose."

Justine finished up her porridge.

"OK, guys, here is the plan. About two hundred metres from here, through the trees, is a building called the White Tower. The Minto family usually operate it as an Airbnb. The geolocation on the Brothel bracelets says the Bunnets are staying there. I'm assuming the five sisters will travel from there to the castle for their weddings. It's walking distance but probably they'll send cars. The wedding is at 10 a.m. so they should be in their wedding dresses and ready at about 9.30. We watch the house from the tree line. If we see they are about to move or if we see anyone from the castle coming down to collect them, we go. The Sheriff and Deputy Chief will take point, because robots are bulletproof. James and Claire, you stay back since you've only got normal kevlar vests."

"Why don't we just grab them now when they are half awake and get out long before the wedding?" asked Claire.

"The Madame asked me to bring them in wearing their wedding dresses," said Justine, "they are going to make a video of us riding up the main street in Pitlochry and use it as a teaser for the TV coverage of the marriage and royal defloration."

"So we're going to hog tie them and throw them over the back of the horse, like in Red Lead Redaction?" asked James.

"No," said Justine. "I tried that with a runaway before and they kept sliding off. We're going to tie their hands in front of them and sit them on the saddle in front of us. If they are stroppy, tie their hands to the saddle horn."

— ♦ —

Justine went to keep watch on the house while the others packed up the camp, saddled the horses, and checked their weapons.

Suddenly Justine appeared from the trees: her mottled fur was such perfect camouflage and her footsteps so light that not even the robots had any warning of her return.

"I can see people in wedding dresses in the front room. There's an older woman at the window staring down the drive like she's expecting someone. I think we have to go. Mount up!"

The posse didn't have the riding skills to gallop or jump walls, so they joined the main trail through the plantation and onto the paved drive which led to the White Tower. They pulled up in the courtyard and drew their guns. Justine ran to the front door.

"Sheriff's Officers! Open up, we have a warrant!"

Ten seconds later, she kicked it in and rushed forward, Glock in hand. The Detective Inspector and Chief Constable took positions outside with long guns covering the driveway. The rest of them ran into the house after Justine.

Mrs Bunnet and her five daughters were gathered in the lounge. With the bay windows, elegant Georgian furniture, and an illegal wood fire, the room could have been a set from a TV costume drama. Four heavily armed Sheriff's Officers dressed as cowboys breaking in on her daughters' wedding day was not part of Mrs Bunnet's plan. But then, neither was getting Tasered.

"Jane, Elizabeth, Mary, Catherine and Lydia Bunnet, you are under arrest. Face down on the floor now. Hands behind your back!"

Then Justine remembered the logistics of taking a prisoner on a horse.

"Sorry, I mean lie on your back, hands in front of you!"

They tied the brides' wrists together with short lengths of rope. Handcuffs would have been easier, but given that the original idea of hog-tying and throwing them across the back of the horse wasn't practical, the Madame had decided tying their wrists with rope was the next best alternative visually. Inconveniently, the dressmakers favoured by the aristocrats did not make such extensive use of velcro as the Brothel's suppliers and the sisters had difficulty mounting the horses. The problem was resolved by Justine cutting a slit in the long skirts with her hunting knife.

The prisoners grasped the pommel of the saddle. The officers mounted behind them and took the reins. They wheeled round and within minutes were back among the trees and heading cross-country towards Aberfeldy. It was a full ten minutes before Justine reported she could hear shouting from the direction of the Tower.

"We've got maybe a fifteen minute lead by the time they get organised. We're on horseback in the forest and they don't know which way we went. As long as we make reasonable time, we should stay ahead easily."

"Don't bet on it. They've got stables and fox hounds at the castle, they'll track you and they'll hang you all," hissed Jane Bunnet. "You have no idea of the power of the Minto family."

As if to drive home her point, a hunting horn sounded from the direction of the castle.

— ♦ —

"They're going to catch up with us," said Justine. "we are two to a horse and some of us aren't experienced riders. Chief, you're the only one without a prisoner. Can you set up an ambush and buy us some time? Remember, PIMPS has the same rules of engagement as Police Scotland. Don't fire unless they are armed or they get close enough that you are in danger from force of numbers. If they have guns, all bets are off and lethal force is authorised."

"Oh, you can be sure they've got guns," said Jane.

"You heard the lady," said Justine, "shoot them."

"Yes Ma'am." said the Sheriff, "That's policy in Amarillo."

The Deputy Chief considered it superfluous to mention that shooting on sight was also Los Espíritus PD policy.

The trail they were following through the forest came to a road. "I've been here before," said Victoria. "On the other side of this road, the trail goes into the Birks of Aberfeldy. There's a waterfall and a footpath down to the town, but we couldn't get the horses down it."

"We're going to have to go cross-country, find our own way, across fields if we need to," said Justine. "They could have people in Aberfeldy by now. We need to skirt around the town on the hillside, and try to stay in the trees and hidden from anyone in the town. Once we get past the town, we'll have to get across the main road without being seen and down to the riverbank, where we can pick up the trail again."

Without a trail to follow skirting round, Aberfeldy was slow work, but they eventually emerged from a field about a kilometre on the other side of town and darted across the main road. It was deserted. No vehicles were moving. They got across the road without being seen and rode over a field to the bank of the River Tay, where they picked up the trail again.

"We just have to follow this trail," said Justine, "in a few kilometres it will move away from the river bank and onto a disused railway line. The trail uses the bridge at Grandtully, which is bound to be watched, so before we get there, we will leave the trail and swim the horses over the river. Once we are across the Tay, it should be safe to use minor roads: they won't be looking for us on that side of the river. We just need to head east until we hit the trail again and can follow it through the forest to Pitlochry."

In the distance, they heard the crack of a gunshot.

"That's a Los Espíritus PD sniper rifle," said James. "Those things never miss. An LEPD sniper in a helicopter can get you with a headshot when you're in a sports car doing 200 kilometres an hour down the freeway."

"I wonder how many of them there are?" asked Claire.

"Fewer than before, that's for sure." said Justine grimly, "Guild robots aren't designed to be sporting. They're designed to aim as fast and as accurately as their hardware allows. And it's damn good hardware. Once they start shooting, it is one shot, one kill. Unless they've got more guys than the Deputy Chief has bullets, that'll be the last we see of them."

"There are a thousand volunteers in the Ath'hole Highlanders," said Elizabeth, "and the other families will also arm their servants and tenants."

"Shit," said Justine, "there's going to be a lot of paperwork."

— ♦ —

They found a suitable point to ford the Tay a couple of hundred metres upstream and out of sight of the bridge at Grandtully. When they reached a minor road following the north bank of the river Justine pulled up to consult the map again.

"It looks good, we just follow this road until it meets up with the trail we were on before, then we cut through a golf course and out onto the open hillside until we hit the forest and then forest tracks down to Pitlochry. There's been no sign of anyone following us and I've not heard gunfire for a while."

WHUMP!

"What in hell was that? It sounded like an explosion," said James.

They looked back and saw a cloud of dust on the horizon.

"That's a Guild robot self-destructing," said Justine, "they've got an explosive charge built in to make sure the technology doesn't fall into the wrong hands. It's not good for anyone close-by when that happens. There'll be a few less pursuers."

"One of your friends is dead!" said Claire. "You don't sound too sad about it."

"His consciousness was uploaded to the cloud years ago," said the Sheriff, "the main copy of the Deputy Chief is still in Los Espíritus and the main copy of me is still in Amarillo. When we make an extra copy of ourselves to download into a telepresence robot it is always temporary. Once you get used to being electronic data and being able to copy yourself you think about these things differently: to all intents and purposes we are immortal."

— ♦ —

There was no sign of pursuit as they rejoined the main trail and rode along the edge of a golf course and out onto the hillside. A stream had burst its banks, and they trotted through flowing water for at least fifty metres, then across a muddy pasture and into the forestry again. They felt safe in the trees, no chance of being spotted by someone with binoculars or one of the aristocrats' retainers with a deer hunting rifle. Soon enough, the path began to descend towards the valley and they caught sight of Pitlochry through the trees. They seemed to have lost their pursuers completely.

The A9, busy with traffic heading towards Inverness at 100 kilometres an hour, was tricky to cross on horseback, but eventually there was a large enough gap. The party crossed the iron suspension bridge over the Tay and they were almost at the station. It was 2.55 p.m., fifteen minutes to spare before the 15.10 to Waverly arrived and no resistance in sight. Mission accomplished.

They hitched their horses outside and Justine went in to buy tickets. There were no railway employees to be seen and the ticket office was locked, but there was an easel with a whiteboard parked strategically in front of it.

"ScotRail apologises for a two-hour delay to the 15.10 to Waverley. This is due to a problem on the line at Blair Atholl."

"Of course it is. Fucking ScotRail!" said James.

"We still need to trot down the high street with the prisoners so the Brothel can get their video," said Justine. "Maybe we can find somewhere to get warm and have a hot drink while we wait for the train."

They rode up Station Road and turned onto the main street, Atholl Road. Townspeople and tourists were taking their phones out to photograph the posse, and there was also a professional photographer with a larger camera on a tripod. One of the hotels had a convenient metal railing, so they hitched their horses and went in to the hotel bar to warm up and get a coffee.

"The Ath'holes are coming!" somebody shouted outside in the street.

The customers started to leave immediately. Drinks were left untouched. In the street people were running into buildings, shops were shutting up. Figures lurked in the shadows, peering out from the bay windows of one building.

"I can hear drums," said Justine, "and bagpipes. Maybe five kilometres away to the North."

The barista was heading for the door. Justine got in front of him and held her hand up.

"Get three coffees ready!" she said from force of habit.

"What do you mean, three coffees?" complained Claire. "There are nine humans and one robot, and the horses deserve a treat too."

"My mistake. Nine coffees."

"And scones," said Victoria. "I think my horse would like a scone."

"OK, OK, nine coffees and a dozen scones. And some jam."

The pipes were getting louder.

"To go."

The barista was trembling. "You're the ones that stole the brides! They'll hang you all for sure. You can't be in here when the Colonel arrives."

"The faster you make our coffee, the faster we leave."

Finally, there were nine coffees on the bar and a paper bag full of scones and little glass jars of jam.

"What's the damage?" asked Justine, taking out her phone.

But before she could pay, the phone in the coffee shop rang. The barista answered.

"They want to talk to you."

"This is Colonel Ruth Lycass of the Ath'hole Highlanders. We have stopped the train at Blair Atholl and we are marching south. Do the right thing and leave the Bunnet sisters in safety and meet us at the Pass of Killiecrankie."

— ♦ —

"Sheriff, we're going to have to fight the Ath'hole Highlanders at Killiecrankie," said Justine, "we can't wait for them to reach Pitlochry and risk civilian casualties."

"That's not good odds," said the Sheriff, "and not an auspicious location for a Claverhouse. You could run away and let me handle it on my own. I'm disposable."

"I'm not running from a fight," said Justine, "but James, Claire and Victoria, I want you to stay here and watch the prisoners and the horses. If the train comes while we are fighting the Ath'hole Highlanders get the prisoners on board."

At that moment, her phone rang. It was Alexandra.

"Hi Alexandra, I'm kind of busy right now."

"Oh, OK, I just wanted to tell you I'm sorry the horse transporter didn't get there before you, but it is just on the edge of town now. It's going to park at the station. Also, I couldn't find any human HGV drivers, so there's a Guild telepresence robot driving it, it's another copy of the Deputy Chief."

"That's great, but…"

"Oh, and I wasn't able to get the police station cab fixed, so it is still stuck at Killin. I'm sorry."

"Don't worry about it…"

"I asked your uncle's Alexandra if we could have a loaner truck while yours is being fixed. I know you didn't want to use anything which had Guild technology, but it was all I could get."

"What did you get, Alexandra?"

"It's your uncle's personal Mobile Operations Centre from the Construction Robotics warehouse at Ratho. It's self driving, should be arriving at the station car park just after the horse transporter. You can unlock it with your phone."

"Alexandra, you are a legend!"

They rode back to the coach park near the train station. The horse transporter was parked off to the side in the space for coaches and beside it was a shiny new articulated lorry. It had no police markings or markings of any kind. It was pure black, and the material had a lustre which was not metallic. Justine recognised it immediately: carbon nanotube armour plating. An armed Guild telepresence robot wearing Los Espíritus PD dress uniform emerged from the horse transporter and walked over.

She took out her phone.

"Hey Siri, open the truck."

"Do you want to use the MOC App function 'unlock'?" asked Siri.

"Yes."

There was a loud clunk as the doors on the cab and the trailer unlocked.

"You two check out the trailer," said the new Deputy Chief, "I'll go in the cab."

Justine and the Sheriff opened the side door and climbed into the trailer. The Chief climbed up into the MOC cab. The trailer was the polar opposite of the old mobile police station. It smelled new. Everything was shiny and brightly lit. They were in a control room: in each corner of the room was a swivel chair with a seat belt facing an array of computer screens, keyboards and joysticks.

The Chief's voice came over the intercom from the cab. "According to the GPS, Killiecrankie is about 5km north, straight up the main road. We can set off whenever you like."

"Go now," said Justine, "the Ath'holes are already on their way. We don't have time to wait."

The Sheriff was pressing buttons on his station at random. Suddenly, the screen lit up.

"Whoah! This thing has drones. This is the control station. I'll try to figure out how it works."

Justine tried pressing the largest button on the console in front of her.

"Mine has CCTV. I'm looking through a camera on the front of the truck."

"There is a cross-hair in the middle of your screen," said the Sheriff, "and this is a Guild vehicle. Be careful until we are out of town!"

"I've got a switch too," said the Chief, "it's big and red."

"May as well press it."

The truck juddered.

"Oh!" said the Chief.

"What just happened?" asked Justine.

"A black box slid out from under the cab. When it was fully extended, it unfolded. Now there's a three-metre-long triangular plough in front of the truck. And armour plates have slid up to cover most of the cab windows. If this thing has bulletproof tyres, it will be unstoppable."

Justine experimented with the joystick on her station and found she could pan and zoom the camera. There was also a large red button under her index finger. They were out of town now: may as well push it.

"Phhhwooomp!" There was a high-tech electrical sound and a tree suddenly burst into flames. A spinning clock icon appeared on her screen along with the word "recharging".

"I've got a laser cannon," said Justine.

The Sheriff had managed to launch a drone and was flying it up the road ahead of the truck.

"There's a drop bomb, option in the drone controls, but I've got no idea what kind of bomb it is carrying."

"Best be careful," said Justine, "with the Guild, it could be anything from a paintball to a tactical nuke."

"Yeah, I'll keep looking through the menus, see if I can get any information."

Things were starting to look a bit brighter.

"Fuck," said the Sheriff, "the drone has reached their column. They've got a tank!"

"What?!"

"They've got an old tank at the front of their column. I think it's a Russian T72. There's a fat woman in army uniform sitting on the turret with one leg on either side of the barrel and shouting orders. Behind her, there are about ten Landrovers with heavy machine guns mounted. After that, it's just infantry. They don't look up to much, but there's a lot of them."

"Don't worry," said the Deputy Chief, "the MOC cab can take 20 rockets, the tank can only take one or two."

"In TDA," said the Sheriff, "but this isn't TDA. There's no guarantee this truck can take a hit from a tank shell. How in the hell did the Ath'hole Highlanders get a T72? I'm sure Queen Victoria didn't sign off on that!"

Justine shrugged. "Colonel Lycass is a Tory. They're always getting dodgy donations from Russia."

"I've found the munitions menu," said the Sheriff, "let's see. Neutron bomb, nerve agent, thermobaric charge, rotary cannon with 30mm depleted uranium shells, cluster munition, white phosphorus..."

"Can we skip past the weapons of mass destruction?" asked Justine.

"Yeah... hold on, anti-tank shaped charge, anti-personnel grenade, land mine, pepper spray, paintball. Most of the illegal ones are greyed out, anyway."

"But what's loaded on the drone now and how many?"

"Don't know. Wait..."

"OK, I think the greyed out ones are ammunition for the on board mortars. The mortars and machine guns are controlled from the other station. The drone is either carrying an anti-tank grenade or pepper spray. I don't know which."

"Drop the fucker on the tank anyway!" suggested the Chief.

"OK, hold on, auto-target... here it goes..."

"It was pepper spray. The tank is undamaged, but there's a cloud of pepper spray over the whole column of infantry. They don't look at all happy."

"Full speed!" said Justine. "Ram the tank and the technicals and scatter the infantry."

"Yes ma'am!"

"The drone is empty. I've ordered it to return and reload and I'm moving to the other station," said the Sheriff.

They were approaching the column now and doing about a hundred kilometres an hour straight down the middle of the A9. The Ath'hole Highlanders opened fire. It sounded like a heavy shower of rain on a slate roof.

"I've got control of the machine guns," said the Sheriff.

"They're not doing any damage," said the Chief, "no need to kill anyone. Wait, the turret on their tank is moving, it's lining up a shot."

"I'm not taking a chance with a tank shell," said Justine. "I'll have to explain any scratches and scrapes to my uncle. Firing laser."

The laser punched a hole in the tank's turret, and its gun stopped moving. Seconds later, the plough on the front of the MOC hit the tank and knocked it to the side of the road. The MOC kept going and crashed through the technicals, tossing them in the air like pebbles. The infantry dived out of the way.

"We're through them," said Justine. "We can turn back."

"The auto-driving computer says the road is too narrow to turn," said the Chief. "GPS is set to go back to Pitlochry, but it's decided to go all the way to Blair Atholl before it turns."

"The computer is probably right. The only way the MOC loses a fight is when you have to turn it and the cab becomes disconnected," said Justine.

"Or the tires get shot out," said the Chief.

"As long as we're going to Blair Atholl, why don't we blow up their castle?" asked the Sheriff.

"Let's just deal with whoever is holding up the train at Blair Atholl," said Justine. "once the train gets to Pitlochry, Ckaire and James will load the Bunnets onto it and the job is done. Akk we need to do is collect the horses and drive down to Edinburgh."

Back up the road, white smoke started to emerge from the tank's turret and billowed around Colonel Lycass. She was starting to think her position straddling the tank gun might have been foolhardy. Sparks started to shoot out near her legs. The ammunition stored inside the turret had been ignited by the laser and was cooking off. Suddenly it exploded and the turret, with the Colonel still straddling it, was thrown into the air with colossal force.

The tank turret was later found two hundred metres away in the middle of a field however, Colonel Lycass was not located. The coroner commissioned a trajectory calculation from the university which concluded that the most likely explanation for the inability to locate her was a secondary explosion of ammunition just as the tank turret reached its apogee acting like a second stage booster and accelerating her beyond escape velocity. Ten years later, this theory was proved correct when her remains were discovered by a Guild Deuterium mining operation on the moon. To this day, Colonel Lycass remains the only Tory politician with a lunar crater named after them.

Five Weddings and a Tribunal

"Sure by Tummel and Loch Rannoch and Lochaber I will go," sang the King on his way down to breakfast, "By heather tracks wi' heaven in their wiles."

The King drank Fuel in the morning like everyone else but his had extra chocolate added by the Palace Chef and it was presented in a golden goblet.

"Good Morning, Sir Philip," said the King to his equerry, "I trust you have called out my men and the west port is unhooked?"

"Yes, Your Majesty, everything is ready for your trip. The Royal Carriage will be coupled to the nine am to Glasgow. We have plenty of time."

"If it's thinkin' in your inner heart the braggart's in my step," continued the King, "You've never smelled the tangle o' the Isles!"

The King was going on holiday. Or rather, he was making an official visit to Skye where he would hold court and preside over a criminal matter which, according to law, could only be judged by the sovereign. A serious business, and one which would be filmed, for a Historic Crimes documentary. The King liked to be on TV, the trip from Glasgow to Skye on the Royal Yacht would be fun but most of all the King was in a good mood because after the trial he could have a week off to walk in the Cuillin and the weather forecast was promising. A whole week of hillwalking was something he'd not managed for a long time, but he'd bagged a hill here and a hill there over his more than twenty-five years as King and he was close to finishing his second round of the Munros.

The King had many impressive orders and decorations, the majority of which he'd given to himself. He had also received distinctions from universities and city councils trying to curry favour and as diplomatic exchanges from other countries. But the achievement he was most proud of was his entry in the records of the Munro Society as a Compleater. Soon he would join the even more select ranks of those who had completed the Munros twice, and this time he intended to do the whole Skye ridge in one push with an overnight bivvy.

The Cuillin Ridge traverse is an impressive tick on the CV of any mountaineer and most would consider it a foolhardy goal for someone approaching their seventieth birthday. However, the King had a few advantages over the majority of his subjects. First, he could afford to pay for professional guides who not only knew the ridge like the back of their hand but would also assist by carrying almost all the equipment and leading any technically challenging sections so the King could follow secured by a rope. The second advantage was that the previous year he had been given a full service by Surgical Robotics Ltd.. His entire body had been imaged and everything which was showing signs of serious wear and tear had been swapped out for brand new 3D printed organs grown from stem cells or, in the case of knees and hips, with mechanically superior components made from advanced materials.

The King was rearing to go and would have preferred to sling on his rucksack and walk to the station, but protocol said he needed to dress up in New Georgian attire and be driven in the royal limousine. The rucksack and hiking gear were hidden away inside a suitcase. He sat in the royal coach and waved for the benefit of the TV as the train pulled out of the station. The royal carriage was so old it didn't even have a holographic projector, and he had to do the waving himself. There were no cheering crowds to see his waves, just some commuters angry at the delay caused by the train operating at restricted speed due to the vintage coach. But the TV would edit in some cheering and some computer-generated crowds and it would all look good on the news. When the train arrived at Glasgow, the Lord Provost was waiting to greet him on the platform with his official car. They made polite conversation on the short drive down to the river where he would join the Royal Yacht.

When the TV company had started work on the project and consulted with Tourism Scotland and Historic Scotland, it had immediately been clear that a Royal visit to Skye by a Jacobite monarch had to be done by sea and the King needed to land at Portree. The very name Portree comes from the Gaelic Port-Righ - Port of the King, it was named following the previous visit of King James V. The problem was the King didn't have a Royal Yacht and the republican-leaning SNP government wasn't about to buy him one. There was, of course, the old English Royal Yacht docked at Leith but it hadn't moved in decades. The engines weren't about to start and nobody was sure it was still seaworthy. And then there was the Waverley. A real, relatively seaworthy, historic paddle steamer. The TV company leased it for two weeks on the spot. The Royal colours were raised, and it became HMY Waverley, and now the King and the Lord Provost were on board with other local dignitaries taking a trip doon the water.

Whenever he came to Glasgow, the King was always taken aback by how much it had changed since the fateful day when he had been deported from Glasgow Airport for overstaying his visitor visa. His anger at the temerity of the English Brexiteers, expelling the last heir of the Stuart dynasty, had led him to join forces with the Guild in a third Jacobite Rebellion, eventually giving up his marketing consultancy in Munich to become king of Scotland. The skyscraper offices of the new financial district lined the north bank of the river, headquarters of the oil companies that had been licensed to open the new fields in the Atlantic and the operators of the wind and tidal energy plants which dotted much of the coastline. At Govan, the naval shipyards of Cockheid Maritime were building frigates and submarines for the EU's Atlantic Fleet. In Greenock, the yards built innovative hydrogen powered ferries for routes to the islands and specialist ships for the offshore wind and oil industries.

Now that Scotland was freed from the shackles of London rule and was able to use its negotiating power as a sovereign country for the benefit of its own industries everything had changed from the situation before independence. The EU wanted to base ships and submarines in Scotland to exert power over the North Atlantic and the quid-pro-quo was to give a fair share of the contracts to construct those ships to yards in Scotland. Energy companies who wanted to exploit Scotland's resources needed to locate top managers in Glasgow, not London. With the senior management, came the spending controlled by senior management.

The Waverley sailed under the new bridge between Greenock and Dunoon and down towards Largs. With the new bridges, Dunoon and Rothesay were becoming attractive satellite towns in Glasgow's commuter belt. As in Norway, main roads now crossed the mouths of sea lochs on bridges and tunnels rather than making the long loop around them. When it reached Knapdale, the last of the peninsulas, the road turned south. Work was already in progress to construct a road tunnel to Ireland to join the existing train tunnel.

Unfortunately, the Waverley, with its paddle wheels, was too wide even for the improved Crinan Canal so it was a long cruise to Tobermory where the King would disembark briefly to declare Archie the Inventor's yellow castle a Historic Monument. He was looking forward to seeing the castle in real life: he had many children and knew every song and episode of Balamory off by heart.

— ♦ —

The following morning the King arrived in Portree and was driven immediately to Dunvegan Castle. That afternoon, the arraignment of Mr Bunnet took place before the court of the King of the Isles in the great hall.

King Charles banged a flagon of mead on the rough wooden table for silence. Mr Bunnet was thrown to the stone floor in front of the throne.

"You are accused of sunshining," said the King, "a pernicious and cowardly trade which I will not abide in my realm. Councillor, consult the book of law and discover the sentence!"

"My Lord. 'In this year 1124, before Christmas, the King sent from Portree and gave instructions that all the sunshiners and anyone whosoever who adulterated the aquae-vitae with base water who were in Skye should be deprived of their members, namely the right hand of each and their testicles below.'"

"Executioner, sharpen your knife!" commanded the King, "and you sirrah, have you anything to say before the sentence is carried out?"

"I wasn't even on Skye," pleaded Mr Bunnet. "I was in Edinburgh!"

"Councillor?"

"The location of the crime is not relevant, Sire. The court has jurisdiction since it was Skye whisky, which was adulterated. However, there is an alternative sentence of a 20,000 euro fine."

"Where am I supposed to find 20,000 euro?" said Mr Bunnet, "My house burned down, I'm skint!"

The King remembered the Campbell trial a few years before and was determined that there would be no actual executions or mutilations in this case if he was involved. He had no problem with a few minutes of dramatic tension, but he'd informed the TV company that if Mr Bunnet refused to pay the fine, he'd issue a Royal Pardon before anything was chopped off. Sure enough, after a suitable pause, a clerk walked over, bowed and handed the King a message.

"I'm informed that by a strange coincidence, your appearance fee for the TV broadcast of these proceedings will be 20,000 euro. Would you like to use that to pay your fine?"

Mr Bunnet thought for a minute. They were clearly trying to railroad him into giving away all his appearance money. But he'd not had that kind of cash for years and he wasn't throwing it away without even rolling the dice.

"I plead not guilty. I want a trial and I'm not paying the fine unless I'm found guilty!"

Several of the islanders present gasped. Silence fell.

"Are you sure?" asked the King.

"Yes, I'm sure. I plead not guilty and I demand a trial."

"Very well," said the King, with a sigh. "Councillor, what does the law book say about trials, bearing in mind that I'm going on holiday tomorrow?"

"There is only one option under the old laws, Your Majesty. The accused must be brought to the Midging Stane at sunset. A truly innocent man has nothing to fear and will survive unscathed until morning."

As dusk fell, Mr Bunnet was driven to the Quiraing at the far north of the Trotternish Peninsula. There he was stripped naked and tied to the column of rock called the Prisoner.

There was no breeze. Only two guards waited to see his fate, safely inside a Land Rover with the windows rolled up.

Mr Bunnet still clung to one desperate hope: the perpetual smell of stale piss which hung around him. Urine contained urea and from what he had read, urea was a midge repellent. And indeed, at first, nothing happened, but then, as he looked out to sea from the Quiraing he saw a black cloud forming. As it approached, it seemed to Mr Bunnet to take an almost human form. Like an aged hag, clothed in black robes and riding on the wind.

But his eyes were playing tricks. It was a swirling cloud of midges. Skye midges. Mainland midges from Cairngorm or Glencoe are fearsome beasties, but even they do not dare venture across the water to Skye. The cloud descended on Mr Bunnet. He felt them crawling on his eyelids and could do nothing to prevent it with his hands tied. He felt them in his nose and his ears and crawling over his testicles. Every time he breathed, he sucked midges into his mouth. Biting and itching and crawling over his whole body and he could not move. He screamed and inhaled even more midges.

The guards too had seen the strange shape riding the wind and, unlike Mr Bunnet, they knew its name. They knew it, but they also knew better than to speak it: Gyre-Carline, NicNevin, Hecate. The Queen of Witches has many names, and it is wiser not to say any of them. But the name which mothers have whispered to generations of recalcitrant children on Skye is by far the most terrifying of all: the Midgepyre.

Within an hour all that was left of Mr Bunnet was a shrunken hulk, every last drop of blood sucked out and so thickly covered in swollen bites that it no longer looked human. The guards dared not approach, even shielded by heavy-duty midge nets, but there was no doubt of the verdict. They called in their report.

"Guilty, Your Majesty."

— ♦ —

After their capture and return to Edinburgh, the Madame was taking no further chances and the Bunnet sisters were confined to VIP suites on the Executive floor of the McLeod International Hotel and Brothel until their marriage. The accommodations were pleasant, but their keycards didn't operate the elevator and all the hotel exits had an alarm which would detect their bracelets if they tried to leave. On the second day of their confinement, Elizabeth received a letter from Skye.

"The Dungeon, Dunvegan Castle, Isle of Skye.

My Dearest Lizzie,

You are by far the most sensible of the family, so I am writing to you. I've been captured by the EDA and taken to Skye, where I will be tried for sunshining tomorrow. I'm not sure how it will go, but there's a chance I won't make it and I want to make sure that you are all fine.

As you know, Jambourn is entailed and since I am the sitting tenant, if I die the Council can evict you and rent it to somebody else. I was talking to the lawyer they brought up here to advise the King, and he said I should put in to buy the property. We have the last council house in Scotland because everybody else has already bought theirs. Apparently, the old Tory right-to-buy laws from before independence say the council has to sell me the house for about a tenth of what it's worth. The lawyer also says it will be worth more now than before it burned down because the site is clear for development. I have filled in the forms and sent them off. Even if they execute me, the application was valid at the point it was made and it will transfer to my estate. The Council can't take the house away as long as you get a 20,000 euro deposit to them by the end of the week.

Also, I think it was that sleekit wee bastard Duke Seuchar that grassed me out to the EDA. Worse than that, I found out he is a director of Hibs. Tell Mary if she marries a Hibee, I'll never speak to her again. I don't care what Mrs Bunnet says, I'll have no Hibees in the hoose, rich or not!

Your loving father,
Mr Bunnet"

— ♦ —

The case against Mr Bunnet was now concluded and the paperwork and evidence needed to be squared away. After receiving a healthy payment from the production company for the Hogmanay Special show, Police Scotland was feeling generous. Even the damage to the traffic car was forgiven after the police were paid extra for the right to include the car camera footage. The Chief Constable personally overruled the accountants and authorised the initial purchases of whisky which had started the investigation to be claimed on expenses. The only downside was the whisky bottles and samples which had been left behind at the arcade needed to be collected, inventoried, and handed over to the evidence store.

Chief Inspector Clark looked out of his window and considered it was far too nice a day for someone as close to retirement as himself to be stuck in an office doing paperwork. Somebody would need to walk round to the arcade on South Bridge and collect the whisky bottles, and it may as well be him. He wasn't sure how much there'd be to carry, but it was possible there'd be too much for one person, so he got one of the historians to come with him. When they got to the arcade, the Chief Inspector saw Justine and her son Robert sitting at the table by the window with ice creams. The ices were a new addition to the cafe's offering, which reflected the increasing influence Mary had over James. Clark knew Justine from her time in Police Scotland as well as from departmental social gatherings she'd attended with Justice Cockburn. He dispatched the constable to buy ices and ask about the whisky bottles, and joined her.

The whisky bottles were easy enough to load into a cardboard crate, but the test tube samples required more careful handling. James had found some bubble wrap and tape and was packing them for transport when the door of the arcade swung open and four men entered. The first was small, thin and had buck teeth. He was wearing a tweed suit and polished brothel-creeper brogues. The other three were large, overweight, and profusely tattooed. James didn't notice their footwear because he was distracted by the baseball bats they were carrying.

The small man walked over to the counter.

"James Fergusson?" he enquired.

"Yes," said James, "this is my arcade. Who are you?"

"I'm Mary Bunnet's fiancé," said Dick Seuchar, "she broke off our engagement and I know you're behind it. You are not going to marry Mary Bunnet. In fact, you are not going to see Miss Bunnet ever again."

"I'll see Miss Bunnet if I want," said James.

"I will make it worthwhile for you to do as I ask, and these gentlemen will make it extremely painful if you do not."

"You can get out of my arcade!"

The man nodded towards the Brothel Lottery terminals on the right side of the room. One of his goons walked over and smashed the screen on the first machine with his bat.

"Perhaps I didn't make myself clear," said the small man and pointed at another of the Brothel's machines.

"Excuse me," said Justine to Chief Inspector Clark, "I won't be a moment."

She walked over to the counter and pulled her PIMP identification badge out of her pocket.

"That lottery terminal is the property of His Majesty's Brothel." she said, holding out her badge.

The historian made to stand up and help Justine but Clark said, "Just sit down, son. Watch and learn."

"Fuck off, bitch!" said the heavy and pushed Justine.

He hadn't expected it to be difficult to push a woman over, but it was much easier than he thought. There was so little resistance, he found himself falling forward. A second later, he noticed that not only was the woman not pushing back, she'd grabbed his arm and was pulling him. She wasn't getting pushed over; she was turning into him. Her free arm had moved up to pin the arm she'd grabbed against her shoulder. She was moving down onto one knee and his momentum was taking him over her back and into the air. Ippon-seoi-nage: one of the first throws Justine had learned, and it was still her favourite.

She wouldn't expect a skilled opponent to walk right into this trap, but with an untrained thug, it was an easy victory, and the move was so much fun to execute perfectly. Her adversary had no time to appreciate the finer points of the throw, because instead of executing a break-fall on a padded mat, he was crashing in an uncoordinated mess onto a hard wooden floor and breaking his collarbone. He didn't remember much after that except a grey blur, which might have been a combat boot approaching his face at high speed. The latter part of Justine's technique wasn't within the rule book of the International Judo Federation but had been highly recommended by her instructors when Europol sent her on the Frontex Special Forces unarmed combat course.

As she rose, Justine grabbed the baseball bat the man had dropped. Without pausing, she drew it back and smashed it into the knees of the second heavy. Double-handed, full force, like she was trying for a home run. The third man turned and ran for the door, but Detective Inspector Clark kicked his feet away from under him and he hit the floor.

"Now, constable, make yourself useful and put on the cuffs."

The small man who'd been giving the orders turned to face Clark. His face was red, but more with anger than fear.

"I am Detective Chief Inspector Clark," Clark held out his ID, "and who are you?"

The man said nothing.

"We can do this at the station if you prefer."

"My name is Richard Seuchar."

"And why were you directing these men to vandalise the Brothel's equipment, Mr Seuchar?"

"I've never seen these men before. I was just about to order a coffee."

The Chief Inspector turned to James. "Do you have CCTV in the cafe, sir?"

"I'm afraid not."

"Well, in that case," Clark drew back his fist and punched Dick Seuchar in the face.

"Resisting arrest," he explained.

— ♦ —

The salubrious Executive Floor of the McLeod International Hotel and Brothel has a shared lounge with free snacks and coffee. Elizabeth had dropped in to collect a coffee and Danish pastry when she heard a sharp voice from somewhere behind her.

"Elizabeth Bunnet, I should like to speak with you!"

She turned and saw a stern-faced lady of about sixty. Her face looked vaguely familiar but Elizabeth couldn't quite place where she'd seen it before.

"How can I help?" she asked civilly.

The woman stood a few feet away and sized her up before replying.

"I must say," she said, "I was expecting someone handsomer. But what do men know of female beauty? In any case, the match is impossible. I forbid it, and you, young lady, would be well advised to desist in your attempts to ensnare Mr Parslikov."

"I'm sorry," said Elizabeth, "but I have no idea who the fuck you are, or, for that matter, what the fuck you are talking about."

"I am Lady Catherine Bampot," she replied, "as you very well know. You should also know that I have considerable power in this country and will shortly have considerably more, and I do not tolerate impertinence."

"Right," said Elizabeth.

"Mr Parslikov is engaged to my daughter, Anne. And, according to the Debutante Draft, you are currently engaged to a certain Mr Fergusson, although that does not seem to trouble you. If you come between Anne and Mr Parslikov, the consequences will be severe. But if you see reason and desist, I am willing to make a financial accommodation with you. I shall require your promise of confidentiality before disclosing the terms.

"I offer no such promise," said Elizabeth proudly. "However, I am prepared to entertain an offer under advisement and without prejudice."

Lady Catherine snorted with anger but decided to make the offer anyway.

"I understand that Mr Fergusson is not a man of means, and your family has an urgent need for money. If you marry Fergusson in the Canongate Kirk on Saturday, I shall pay your mother two hundred thousand euro."

"That's a really good offer for a girl like me," replied Elizabeth, "but I want the fairy tale."

"Stupid girl!" snapped Lady Bampot. "Perhaps you fancy yourself in love with Mr Parslikov?"

"Perhaps I do," replied Elizabeth.

"You will bring nothing but dishonour and disgrace to him. The Parslikovs are a proud Russian family. For a Russian, there is no greater dishonour than watering down spirits. The daughter of a sunshiner will never be welcomed into polite society. My offer remains open: two hundred thousand euro to clear your mother's debts if you marry Mr Fergusson."

Lady Catherine turned on her heel and left, leaving Elizabeth in a whirl of conflicting emotions. Was it fair to repay Arseny for restoring Lydia's reputation by tarnishing his own family name with a marriage to the daughter of a sunshiner?

— ♦ —

"James, you've got a letter," said Claire.

James looked up from his computer.

"What d'you mean," he replied, "I'd get a notification if I had e-mail."

"You've got an actual paper letter," she said. "A woman in Brothel uniform came out of the Dishonesty Box and handed it to me."

She was holding the corner of the letter between the nails on her thumb and index finger to minimise the contact with her skin and, rather than hand it over, she placed it on the desk in front of him.

"Euuugggh," said James, "it's written on bog paper!"

Nevertheless, he was curious enough to unroll the missive and begin reading. Claire looked over his shoulder.

"Dear James, *I hope this finds you well. I apologise for the stationery. The brothel has locked us up until we are married. It isn't too bad, it's one of the rooms they use with clients, so there's a nice bed and a toilet but the door is locked, there's no computer and they've taken my phone. There was a free 'H.M. Brothel' pen in the room for customers to take as a souvenir, but all I have to write on is toilet paper. Don't worry, I used a fresh bit."*

"It's OK, she used a fresh piece," said James to Claire.

"I'm still going to wash my hands!"

James continued reading.

"You probably think I am a bitch for agreeing to marry Arseny, even though he hadn't made a trade with you. I didn't have any choice. I only had one offer. Arseny was going to give my mother 100,000 euro immediately after we were married. With all five of us, she would have had 500,000 euro and could have paid off her debt. If my mother doesn't pay off her debt in the next week, the brothel will call in our guarantee and the five of us will be the prize in the Brothel Lottery for October."

"She should still have made him trade with you," said Claire, "and he shouldn't have tried to maroon you on his yacht."

"I don't blame you for helping the bounty hunters, but I am now in a terrible position. Lady Catherine Bampot visited me. She is livid about me marrying Arseny. She says she'd been talking to Arseny about marrying her daughter Anne for years and he suddenly changed his mind a few days ago when he met me."

"That's the girl Justine caught cheating at the cheese competition," said Claire, "serves her right if she's lost her man."

"Lady Catherine says if I marry you, instead of Arseny, she will pay my mother 200,000 euro. I know it is a lot to ask, but I was wondering if we could get back together? I have no personal conditions. I'm not asking for any money. You just need to turn up in Canongate Kirk the day after tomorrow and say 'I do'. Love, Elizabeth."

"She's got a cheek," said Claire. "After all that, she expects you to marry her the day after tomorrow."

"P.S. Assuming we get married, Jane and Mary are asking if we'd be interested in husband swapping this weekend."

Claire watched James's face unwind from a frown to a smile as he read the last sentence.

"You know," she said, "as a student of romantic fiction, it never ceases to amaze me how many of the dilemmas faced by characters could be resolved by bisexuality, wife swapping and polygamy."

"What did you say?" asked James.

Claire started to repeat herself, but he cut her short.

"Never mind! I've worked it all out. I'm going to need some bog roll and a pen!"

— ♦ —

The day of the Bunnet sisters' wedding arrived. The weather forecast was excellent, the skies were blue, and the council had sent out a fleet of robotic cleansing vehicles to spruce up the path of the procession. Barriers had been placed to hold back the crowds, the Scottish Broadcasting Corporation was ready with cameras on cranes and drones to cover every metre of the route, and the King's equerry was issuing shotguns to the footmen who would provide a bridal guard of honour. The wedding convoy formed up on Alex Salmond Bridge outside the City Farm's Cafe. First three motorcycle outriders from Police Scotland, next a Brothel PIMP patrol vehicle with a crew of armed officers, then the flatbed truck with the five transparent Prisoner Transport Units which held the five brides, next the five limousines conveying the five grooms and finally three more motorcycle outriders. The flatbed truck was the last to arrive, taking its place in the convoy after loading up at the prisoner entrance to the courts.

Jane had not envisaged being driven to her wedding in a cell on the back of a truck. She'd hoped for a vintage Rolls Royce like the one at Taymouth Castle, but she'd have settled for a Mercedes. However, the cheering crowds which lined the Royal Mile as the brides were delivered from the Brothel's detention suite at the Courts to Canongate Kirk made up somewhat for the ignominious mode of transport and she made the best of it and smiled and waved. Her dress had been carefully mended and dry-cleaned and the Brothel had employed the city's best hairdressers and make-up artists to work their magic. She had to admit that the two-metre high transparent cage gave the crowds a far better view of her finery than a small window in the back of a car. The wedding video would be spectacular.

The convoy moved slowly, but the route was only a little more than a kilometre and soon enough, they reached their destination.

The grooms went into the church and waited by the altar while the robotic arm on the back of the Brothel's truck lifted the Prisoner Transport Units off and placed them carefully on the ground. Sir Philip McCann, the King's equerry, signed the delivery receipt and five footmen from the palace with hand trolleys came forward to collect the brides. They pushed the tines of their trolleys into the slots under the prisoner transport units, pulled back to lift them off the ground and wheeled them down the aisle as the organist played 'Here Comes the Bride'.

After a brief protest from the minister, the brides were handcuffed and allowed to leave their cells during the service. Jane was so happy she forgot about the handcuffs and the ceremony flew past in a blur. The church was beautiful. Her mother was in the front row of the congregation and she had made the match of her dreams. Later, all she could remember was saying 'I Do' and the ring being placed on her finger. Her sisters were making their vows on either side of her. She placed her finger on the minister's iPad to sign the legal documents, and it was a done deal. She was a married Lady. Not just a lady, but a Lady with a capital letter, the wife of a baronet. The minister congratulated the couples, the final hymn was sung and the choir processed off the altar. Silence fell in the church.

The King's equerry and a squad of footmen from the palace marched up the aisle. Each footman carried a shotgun slung over their shoulder in case of trouble.

"Nice day for it," said Sir Philip to the minister by way of conversation.

"If you don't have to start again!" said the minister, "I've got two more weddings straight after this one."

While they were talking, the footmen loaded the brides back into their cells and started off down the Royal Mile to the palace.

The grooms stood in front of the altar, not sure what to do with themselves now their brides had been wheeled away.

"Come on then," said Sir Philip, "you're invited too."

"What d'you mean?" asked Baron Minto.

"It's 2047," said Sir Philip, "there are sex discrimination laws! Obviously, Jus Primae Noctis applies to the husbands as well as the wives."

"For fuck's sake," said Trevor, "It's bad enough the King deflowering my wife. I didn't sign up for this shit!"

"Hold on," said Whackov, "maybe there's a get-out. Doesn't Jus Primae Noctis, only apply to virgins?"

Ross perked up for a second then realised he was still fucked.

"Technically, yes," said Sir Philip angrily. "However, the Queen has reorganised her schedule specially and is waiting for you in the palace. It would be extremely disrespectful to Her Majesty not to show up."

Grumbling, the five grooms followed Sir Philip and the procession of footmen to the palace.

Noblesse Oblige.

— ♦ —

The City of Edinburgh, aforetime and now restored capital of Scotland lay between the Pentlands and the Forth in all the brightness of a September morning. The sun glinted on the sloping High Street from the Castle to the Palace and a light mist rose as it dried the last dampness of a brief shower. From the grassy meadow near the Parliament, as every native of Edinburgh knows, a rough path ascends at the base of the crags and provides an unrivalled outlook over the city.

It was on this Radical Road that two female figures were walking rapidly, their breath coming fast and colour rising to their cheeks and heads bent with the effort of ascending the steep incline. One of the pair was Claire and the other, a fine budding figure, with beautiful eyes, Victoria. When they had reached the top of the rise above the parliament, the clock of the Balmoral Hotel struck twelve. They both started at the sound, walked another few steps and sat on the turf at the margin of the path, and impelled by a force that seemed to overrule their will, stared out over the city.

The prospect from their vantage point was almost unlimited. The wide Forth Estuary, and beyond it the hills of Fife. The yachts moored in Leith, the superyacht Admiral Pemberlov, too large to enter the port, moored near Inchkeith island. The Parliament and the Castle. But their eyes were drawn to none of these structures. Below them, in the Park, Holyrood Palace stood within its carefully tended grounds and on its roof, the Lion Rampant, the Royal Standard, flew, streaming out in the light breeze. Next to it, a smaller mast had been raised, no flag flew from it but it was on this erection the gaze of the two ladies was concerned. Their eyes were riveted on it.

A full thirty minutes after the hour had struck, a liveried footman appeared on the roof. A pair of white lacy panties moved slowly up the flagpole and extended themselves on the breeze. Justice was done, and the King had ended his sport with Jane.

The two speechless gazers settled themselves down with beer and popcorn. They remained thus, while the panties continued to wave silently from the roof of the palace below. As the hours progressed, a second, a third and fourth pair of virginal white undergarments joined them.

The sun was setting when the footman ascended to the palace roof for the final time. But this time the underwear raised on the flagpole was not pristine white but maroon, with 'JAM TARTS' spelt out in block capitals across the rear.

"Lydia!" said Victoria and Claire at almost exactly the same time.

The Happy Ending

After the deflorations concluded, the King hosted a reception for the brides and their families in the palace.

James and Arseny walked down from the bedrooms after changing their clothes. Both had a somewhat unusual gait.

Arseny gave James a fist bump. "Well, I have to admit, your crazy idea worked. I'll be walking funny for a month, but it was worth it. Elizabeth is still a virgin."

"I knew it would," said James. "The law is clear. The King must deflower the bride and the Queen the groom. As soon as we swapped gender identities, the girls were safe from the King's attentions."

Elizabeth extracted a grey pubic hair from her molars.

"Safe from the King, maybe!"

"What about the second part of the plan?" asked Arseny.

James and Elizabeth checked their phones.

"Dick Seuchar's lawyers have wired me 100k because I didn't marry Mary."

"And Lady Catherine has wired me two hundred because I didn't marry Arseny," said Elizabeth, "Along with a hundred from the Murrays and another from the Mintos my mother will be able to pay off her loan and our guarantee won't be called in."

Arseny laughed. "The richer I become, the more I enjoy getting things for free. I could easily have paid myself, but this is so much more satisfying."

They hadn't noticed that Lady Bampot had drawn closer to their group and was listening to everything they said.

"Very amusing Miss Bunnet," she said, "of course I honoured the agreement I signed. Under normal circumstances, I would have made sure you regretted crossing me. However, in this case, your little scheme worked out in my favour."

Elizabeth blushed deeply.

"Yours was not the only marriage in the Canongate Kirk this afternoon," said Lady Bampot.

"Did Charlie manage to marry McCallister?" asked Elizabeth. "I thought her arse was still in a sling?"

"It is indeed. Nevertheless, the marriage went ahead, but I imagine it will be some time before it can be consummated. However, theirs are not the nuptials I was referring to. My daughter Anne was married to Dick Seuchar. It is a most advantageous match."

"Congratulations," said Elizabeth, "they share so many interests, I'm sure they will be happy."

The King was circulating around the room and joined their party.

"I pride myself on being open-minded," said the King to Arseny and James, "but I must confess that I was initially disappointed when I discovered that two of the brides were biologically male. Our encounter greatly exceeded my expectations. Nevertheless, I suspect the Queen might have had the better of the arrangement. I am led to believe Miss Elizabeth Bunnet is a skilled performer."

"Her performance was pleasing, but by no means capital," replied Lady Catherine Bampot, cooly. Lady Catherine was the first wife of the King which made her the senior queen of Scotland - there were, of course, many others.

"My fingers," said Elizabeth, "do not move over that organ in the masterly manner which I see so many women's do. They have not the same force and rapidity and do not produce the same expression. But then I have always supposed it to be my own fault, for I do not take the trouble of practising."

"In my opinion, Miss Bunnet would not play at all amiss, if she practised more and would have the benefit of a London Master," said the Madame, who had also joined their group, "She has a very good notion of fingering, though her taste is not equal to Anne's."

"Anne was an exceptionally cunning linguist," said Lady Bampot. "She might well have achieved a gold medal in that event to go with her bronze had the team not instructed her to retire."

"Injury," said the Madame, "is a hazard in any sport. In my view, the physio made the right decision. It would have been foolhardy to continue with a seriously sprained tongue."

Lady Catherine continued her remarks on Elizabeth's performance, mixing them with many instructions on execution and taste until the King, seeing that Miss Bunnet was growing weary of her Ladyship's imprecations, called for the attention of the gathering.

"It seems only fair to toast the marriages of the Bunnet sisters with the last of my Morningside Mist," said his Majesty. "I regret I only have half a bottle left from the supply I purchased from the late Mr Bunnet, so the portions will be small."

His Majesty filled their glasses himself.

"To the brides and grooms!" he said, raising his glass, and the company followed.

After the toast, the King managed to break away from Lady Catherine and join the Bunnets. He looked around to make sure that no one was close enough to overhear.

"I suppose there is no chance that you could resume production?" he asked.

"Dad got caught," said Kitty. "If we start again, the EDA will know exactly where to look. We'd need a brand new plan."

"Why don't you just buy the whisky?" asked the King. "There's no need to continue your father's sunshining scheme. I'm sure the Murrays or the Mintos could sell you some suitable spirits from their Speyside distilleries. If it was made legally, I would issue a Royal Warrant."

Trevor Minto savoured the last of his Morningside Mist.

"If this was made using whisky from our distillery in Aberfeldy and it had a Royal Warrant, I could sell perhaps fifty or a hundred bottles a week at one thousand euros a bottle in the European market alone."

"It's not just getting the whisky legally," said Mary. "The cream comes from goat's milk. We tried human milk, but the taste isn't the same."

"If you don't mind me asking," said Mrs Bunnet to Elaine, "how did you manage to get New Lanark cheese made from human milk to taste exactly like the original made from cow milk?"

"My daughter Hestia helped," said Elaine proudly. "She altered the DNA of the bacteria, which makes the cheese so it could work with human milk."

"That's clever," said Mary, "but it won't work for Morningside Mist because there are no bacteria involved in making cream."

"True," said Justine, "but there are more tools in the biochemistry toolbox than tinkering with mould bacteria. It might be possible."

After the reception broke up, and she was leaving the Palace with Elaine, Justine called Alexandra.

"Hi, Alexandra,"

"Are you having fun at the palace? Is Morningside Mist as delicious as they say?"

"It smells like it would be delicious, but I haven't tasted it. I'm lactose intolerant. Cat DNA."

"That's a shame!"

"Anyway Alexandra, we were talking about Morningside Mist and I was thinking that maybe we could make the goat's milk cream legally from human milk if we used Guild technology like we did for the cheesemaking. I'd like to ask my aunt for some chemistry advice, but I don't want to disturb her. Does she have a copy of herself on your system you could ask?"

"Oh, yes, Dr Dickson always has a few copies of her process working on some project or other. Hold on, I'll ask one of them."

As usual, Alexandra had the answer immediately, inter-processor communication being far faster than human speech.

"Dr_Dickson_00053 says the chemistry is not difficult, and she thinks it would be a good practical exercise for you after you finish the next module in your course. She says you can borrow the equipment from the farm again, but you are not to ask Hestia for help and she will know if you do."

Justine turned to Elaine. "Well, my aunt says human milk can be turned into goat cream, but she's not told me how to do it and I'm not allowed to ask Hestia. She says it's an exercise."

"If you don't mind me saying so, that was a rookie mistake," replied Elaine. "Ask a teacher to solve a problem, and all you get is homework. Ask a student and they'll do the work for you for free to prove they can. You should have gone straight to Hestia like I did."

— ♦ —

After exchanging phone numbers with the King, the couples left the palace through a side gate. Cars were waiting to take Jane and Trevor to their estate and Lydia and Whackov to the airport. Kitty and Ross Murray only had the short walk up the Royal Mile to Canongate Manse.

James and Elizabeth followed Arseny and Mary in the opposite direction, along the lane which led to Holyrood Park. A blue Eurocopter was waiting on the lawn near the palace. Arseny opened the cabin door for his guests. Soon they had taken off and were heading out to sea.

"I have the captain waiting on the Admiral Pemberlov to conduct the ceremonies," said Arseny, "Now we have swapped back to our usual genders James can take Mary as his second wife and I can take Elizabeth as mine and everything will be as it should be."

"A blended double thrupple," said James.

James's phone began to ring. It was his friend Alexandra.

"Hi Alexandra, I'm just off to be married again," he said.

"I know. I can track your phone and your brothel bracelet."

"Oh, yes, I forgot that. How can I help?"

"I was wondering, did you and Arseny do that thing with the gender swaps just so that Mary and Elizabeth wouldn't get pregnant?"

"Yeah, of course," said James proudly. "It was a brilliant plan, wasn't it?"

"Well, just so you know, Professor McTavish asked for the contraception on the Bunnet sister's MedChips to be turned on months ago. She's blocking the Murrays, Mintos and Seuchars from having heirs because the landowners paid someone to kill her."

"What!? How can she do that? I thought they were special Italian MedChips."

"All MedChips are controlled by the MedChip corporation servers. It makes no difference if they were sold to the Scottish or Italian governments. Dr Knox's Alexandra runs all those systems. I can ask her to change the settings for Mary and Elizabeth if you want."

James checked with Mary and Elizabeth.

"Maybe in a few years, Alexandra, but I think it would be best to leave the contraception on for now."

— ♦ —

Mrs Bunnet and the five sisters stood outside the remains of Jambourn. The house had been demolished, and the rubble cleared away. Mrs Bunnet now lived in a caravan parked where Mr Bunnet's shed had once stood. All six ladies were dressed in black and Mrs Bunnet was carrying a specially commissioned urn with the ashes of her late husband. The urn was maroon and bore the famous Heart of Midlothian logo. Mrs Bunnet had almost dropped it in shock when she collected it, having misread HMFC as HMRC at first glance. It was time for Mr Bunnet's last journey.

A cortege of fifty ice-cream vans lined Craigmillar Castle Road all the way from Niddrie Mains Road to the castle. The Bunnet's van was parked in front of their property. The family packed in, Elizabeth was driving and Mrs Bunnet, as usual in the passenger seat. The urn was given the place of honour, on display behind the serving hatch. The lead van turned on its chimes, the other vehicles followed suit, and the convoy departed. Mrs Bunnet was moved to tears. Everything had changed. Her daughters were married, her debt was discharged, but all that remained of her husband and her beautiful house, Jambourn, was a Jambo urn.

Accompanied by a respectful escort of police motorcycle outriders, the procession made its way towards the centre of town. They turned along the Meadows and down Lothian Road to the Western Approach Road. Soon they were approaching their destination. By this time, the police and management of Heart of Midlothian FC had also deduced the intentions of the convoy. A roadblock was set up at the entrance to the ground, but the cortege came to a stop before reaching it at a lay-by on the Western Approach Road. The vans at the front and back, pulled out, blocking the road in both directions. Dusk was falling as Mary Bunnet opened the serving hatch on the family van and launched a quadcopter drone into the air, the urn with the ashes of her late father suspended under it. The drone flew north over Tynecastle Stadium and when it was directly above the centre circle of the park, rose high into the air, navigation lights flashing in the darkening sky.

The assembled ice-cream vans played 'Highland Cathedral' on their chimes as the drone hovered above the centre of Tynecastle Park. As the music ended, the urn was released and tumbled towards the earth. A second into its flight, there was a flash of light, a loud bang, and streams of sparks cascaded outwards.

The sparkles from the firework faded and Mr Bunnet's ashes fell like maroon rain over the hallowed ground as the pokey hat men raised 99 cones in a final salute.

Author's Note

Dear Reader,

Thank you for reading 'Once Upon a Time in Holyrood'. I hope you enjoyed it as much as I enjoyed writing it!

As you probably noticed sections of this book are a parody or pastiche of 'Pride and Prejudice' by Jane Austin, the movies 'Top Gun' and 'Pretty Woman' and the song 'Copperhead Road'. There are also scenes inspired by 'The Laird of Cockpen', 'Macbeth', and 'Tess of the d'Urbervilles'.

If you're interested in Easter Egg hunts, buried throughout the text there are quotations from the original 'Pride and Prejudice': some have small changes to make them fit with the sentences around them. How many can you find?

I usually try to keep the location descriptions accurate: for example, the Western Town and the Arcade's location with the secret room hidden in the bridge are real places in Edinburgh and the route Justine and the bounty hunters take between Edinburgh and Pitlochry is based on the Rob Roy Trail. However, I took some liberties in this book for plot reasons. There is currently no motor museum on the Museum of Flight campus at East Fortune Airport. The Lotus Elite from the James Bond movie 'The Spy Who Loved Me' is in Scotland in a display of cars from the movies but it is in the Bo'ness Motor Museum.

Work has already started on the next book in the series which is provisionally titled 'No Comets Seen.'

Keep up with the series on Twitter @rassleagh or Facebook https://www.facebook.com/sean.t.rassleagh.

All the best,
Sean.

Catch Up

If you're starting this book before reading the previous novels in the Future Edinburgh series here is a brief and spoiler-free catch-up on the Edinburgh of 2047.

In 2024 a secret society of Edinburgh University scientists called the Guild colluded with the Vatican to stage a third Jacobite rising and used advanced technologies to defeat the Viceroy imposed by Westminster and obtain independence. Scotland is now an independent country within the EU. The monarch in these books, King Charles, is the last surviving heir of Bonny Prince Charlie, not Charles Windsor. Some streets have been renamed, replacing the names of Hanoverian English monarchs with famous Scots.

Following a disastrous hurricane which destroyed their headquarters in New York, the United Nations agreed a series of treaties to mitigate climate change. Farming animals was banned to reduce the emissions of greenhouse gasses from agriculture and licences are required to have children. Global warming has changed Scotland's climate, storms are more frequent, and sea levels have risen. Edinburgh has built a new sea wall in the Forth, it has also extended the Union Canal all the way to the sea at Portobello, restored the Nor'Loch in Princes Street Gardens and built new drainage canals to deal with flooding.

Before independence, the Tory government in Westminster experimented with privatising the prison system and licencing prisons to run as brothels so they could turn a profit. This has never been reversed by the Scottish Government. With increased automation income tax revenues are falling and more and more of the government's revenue is coming from fines imposed by the justice system. Despite farming animals being banned the rich still demand dairy products and this has created a market for human milk which provides a secondary source of revenue from the penal system.

Despite the economic difficulties people are healthier and live longer than ever before thanks to technologies provided by Guild-associated companies. Everyone has a MedChip implanted within their body which monitors their health, it can also control pain to a limited degree, provide contraception and dispense some medications. The MedChips work in conjunction with a drink called Fuel which is provided by the NHS. Fuel is individually formulated based on a person's DNA, medical history and data from their MedChip to provide tailored nutrition and medication.

The Greens have been the minor party in the governing coalition for almost thirty years. As a result, there has been a raft of legislation on political correctness and social issues. Polygamy has been legalised and people can change the gender they wish to identify as whenever they like using a setting on their phone. Many people have both a female and a male first name to make this more convenient.

Table of Contents

Once Upon a Time in Holyrood	1
Copyright and Warning	2
The Bunnets	3
Sunshiners	24
The Debutante Draft	41
Morningside Mist	68
The Ball	80
Wild Mountain Time	96
Marooned	110
15:10 to Waverley	134
Five Weddings and a Tribunal	155
The Happy Ending	171
Author's Note	177
Catch Up	178

Printed in Great Britain
by Amazon